A Virtue of Marriage

THE SECOND BOOK OF THE MORALITIES OF MARRIAGE SERIES

Elizabeth Ann WEST

© 2015, Elizabeth Ann West. All rights reserved.

To contact the publisher, please write to

41 Silas Deane Road

Ledyard, CT 06339 or email

<u>writer@elizabethannwest.com</u>

ISBN-13: 978-1511411363
ISBN-10: 1511411368

Happiness in marriage is a matter of chance.
Jane Austen

Acknowledgments

This novel series would not be possible without the love and kind support of the Jane Austen Fan Fiction community. I am a proud author member of Austen Authors and love working with all of my brothers and sisters writing JAFF! Our genre rocks!

The readers at TheCheapEbook.com are also wonderful friends of my writing and without them, my launches would fall flat on their faces! The "Piggies" are savvy readers with hearts of gold.

To my best friend and #1 pusher to make me do great things, April Floyd, I am indebted to you. You are a superstar and I am lucky to have you to call at all hours of the day!

Finally, to my husband who supports me 110%, my super stepson who tells anyone and everyone his mother is an author, and to my five-year-old daughter who insists I do not write stories, I type them, thank you. Mommy couldn't do this without you.

Always Smiling,
Elizabeth Ann West

ALSO BY ELIZABETH ANN WEST

AUSTEN INSPIRED

By Consequence of Marriage
What if Darcy never saved Georgiana from the clutches of Wickham? First novel in the Moralities of Marriage series.

The Trouble With Horses
Darcy falls off a horse, Elizabeth saves him and the whole town is talking about it! A sweet historical romance novella.

A Winter Wrong
First book in the Seasons of Serendipity novella series. When Mr. Bennet dies of an epidemic, Elizabeth Bennet learns that the kindness of a stranger can be quite dashing! A sweet, historical romance novella.

A Spring Sentiment
Second book in the Seasons of Serendipity novella series. It's going to take all of the Bennet sisters to get Mr. Darcy and Elizabeth to march down the wedding aisle!

A Summer Shame
Third book in the Seasons of Serendipity novella series. The honeymoon trip of Darcy and Elizabeth is a crowded affair and Jane learns London Society is a scandal waiting to happen.

An Autumn Accord
Fourth book in the Seasons of Serendipity novella series. Darcy and Elizabeth mark the one-year anniversary of her father's death by returning to Hertfordshire where the Widow Bennet has a new problem to share.

OTHER TITLES

Cancelled
Original novel, a modern romance told mostly from the male point-of-view. A robotics engineer becomes engaged to his perfect match when a previous one-night stand shows up to return his shirt. Pregnant. And it's his.

Visit the *Rose Room*, an exclusive reading club, for more information and to read free stories. Available free at http://elizabethannwest.com/roseroom

To our future selves, the glory is in the work.

Chapter One

Charlotte Collins plucked more lavender sprigs from the partially shaded corner of her garden, placing long stems of the herb into her white apron. The quick pace formed perspiration under her many layers of clothing, but she would not remove her bonnet lest Mr. Collins return early from his constitutional walk. Her loose hair proved an easy distraction to her toad of a husband.

A dust cloud followed a hastily driven carriage down the lane. The man inside took little notice of the small woman gathering herbs in her garden. Charlotte squinted her eyes at the coach and recognized the equipage. Catching her breath, she hurried to complete her work.

Married to Mr. Collins for three months, she needed to collect and dry as many stems as she could. If she made enough soap for the household, perhaps she could sell some in town for a minor profit. Her husband was always crossest over the lack of funds for their family. At twenty-seven, Charlotte had been long considered "on the shelf," and her father, a lowly baronet in Hertfordshire had redirected most of her dowry. The day her marriage settlement was signed ended most of the goodwill she had experienced previously from her intended.

"My wife, was that not Mr. Darcy's carriage just now in the lane?"

Charlotte cringed. She was caught. The last thing she wished to do was talk about Mr. Darcy. Not to Mr. Collins; not to anyone. Since he had arrived with Lady Catherine two months ago, there had been nothing but strife. Lady Catherine's moods shifted as frequently as a windmill turns, with her husband bearing the brunt of her moments of displeasure. In turn, Charlotte bore the brunt of Mr. Collins' displeasure.

"I believe so, Mr. Collins."

"Did you not rise and curtsy as I have instructed you?"

Charlotte stood hastily with her apron corners in hand, unfortunately pulling the corner of her work gown slightly askew, revealing a well-formed, stockinged right calf. She witnessed Mr. Collins' stare of desire before quickly reaching down and settling her skirts to fall properly. Marching to the back door of the cottage, Mr. Collins blocked her way.

"Mrs. Collins, perhaps you are fatigued from your morning's endeavors and care to join me in a rest? For your health of course." The man licked his lips and inhaled a deep breath.

The stench of his body odor, pungent from his hasty rush to greet a carriage he had no hope of meeting, made her revile at his invitation. "I feel quite well, thank you," she managed.

"Yet, you did not stand to greet Mr. Darcy as I have implored you to honor all of the illustrious persons of Rosings. The worthy name of our patroness, and her relations, deserve the reverence of nobility. I presumed you too fatigued to stand or you would obey your husband." Mr. Collins piety began to bring an irritated tone to his voice. But he was no match for Charlotte.

She bowed her head and slowly raised her eyes to look through her long lashes. "You are correct, sir, that I am unwell with the plague women must bear. I was gathering herbs so that I might brew a tea to lessen these symptoms. I have failed to fulfill my duty to Mr. Darcy's carriage, but I only did so in hopes of fulfilling my duty to you."

Mr. Collin's tongue made an unflattering flapping sound. Charlotte knew well when she had appealed to her husband's baser nature in order to, once again, absolve her of that particular wifely duty. In this case, she even succeeded in alleviating her guilt for purposely ignoring her husband's command to curtsy for a rushing coach.

Realizing Mr. Collins needed prompting, she used her best tone of deference. "Sir, might I make myself a cup of tea? I shall sit and plan this week's meals with Cook."

Snapping to attention, Mr. Collins nearly jumped out of his wife's way so she could enter the kitchen. Leaving him in the doorway, she joined Mrs. Plummer, the cook, and deposited her pullings carefully into a bin. Mrs. Plummer handed Charlotte the twine and wiped her hands from the stew she was stirring. The two women spied through the small window that Mr. Collins continued to walk through the garden to the other side of the property in a direction to check on his beehives.

"Have the eggs been collected from the coop?" Charlotte grabbed a bunch of the pale purple thistle-like blooms and wrapped a cord of twine around the base before tying the bunch to a nail in the windowsill.

"Yes, ma'am. Eileen found three eggs this morn."

"Three? Mrs. Plummer do we not keep ten chickens?"

Mrs. Plummer looked down at her own bundle and quickly tied it off. "Rightly, you do. But for the life of me, this past week the eggs have been scarce, ma'am. It might be from that last spring storm."

Charlotte pursed her lips. She highly doubted spring storms were spooking the chickens, at least she'd never seen such a thing at Lucas Lodge, her father's estate. No, Charlotte suspected a much more sensible reason her eggs were missing, and as Mistress of Hunsford Lodge, she intended to discover the cause.

"See that the stew does not scorch. Mr. Collins is unbearable in the evenings when his dinner does not settle well." Charlotte left the kitchen to hurry upstairs and freshen up. She was to walk to Rosings and perform her daily visit with Anne de Bourgh as she had done every day since a week after her arrival.

The cook nodded, knowing Mrs. Collins meant no disrespect. The three weeks she had been employed at the parsonage she had watched her new mistress dodge the master's advances enough to value Charlotte as one smart woman. The entire household pitied the woman forever tied to Mr. Collins, both here and the thereafter, in holy matrimony.

Chapter Two

Fitzwilliam Darcy entered Rosings covered in dust and walked straight to the gaudy sitting room, knowing he'd find his aunt there, never next to her daughter's sickbed. The walls held so many ornamentations and ancient tapestries, it was a dark and dank room, and Fitzwilliam's least favorite.

"Fitzwilliam, thank goodness you have come. Anne has taken to her bed once more and Dr. Sneads is certain her time is near." Lady Catherine lacked any maternal concern in her voice and did not rise from the overly ornate wingback chair she used as an impromptu throne.

"I shall see to my betrothed, presently, once I am changed. Madam." Darcy bowed and tried to exit the parlor.

"Don't open that door!" Lady Catherine instructed the poor footman. "Whatever did you need to rush to Pemberley for? You never satisfied my question before you abruptly departed two weeks ago. What if Anne had died? You must marry right away, this very afternoon!" Lady Catherine barked her orders from her pretender's throne.

Darcy clenched his teeth. For two months he had stalled and stymied his family's attempts to make him wed his sickly cousin, Anne. First, he delayed their arrival as long as he could with matters in London. Then, he spent weeks pouring over the accounts of Rosings, justifying the action as necessary to reconcile the marriage settlement papers. Then he made certain to find a mistake and return to London under the charade of seeing his solicitor. Finally, he used Pemberley as an excuse. But time marched on. He was running out of excuses to delay the wedding.

Richard was to have procured leave a month ago and arrive for the switch in groom, but his military duties continued to thwart their plans. The only sustenance that allowed Darcy to endure night after night of his aunt's rude, brash manner was the handful of love letters from his true love, Elizabeth Bennet. The two brief times he managed to go to London, he saw his secretly betrothed, but her uncle, Edward Gardiner, refused to allow them any privacy.

Darcy couldn't blame the man; his situation remained precarious and should something happen, Elizabeth would be alone.

"I explained that I saw to the preparations of the mistress suite at Pemberley. If a man is to take a wife, there are certain preparations that must be met. I had planned to stop off in London to see that home, but your missive said Anne was dying." He didn't add that he instructed the decorations based on the Elizabeth's tastes, not Anne's.

"She is! Her doctor assures me there is precious little time and one more illness will take her away! Marry and be done with it, you can have your bits of muslin on the side." Lady Catherine waved her hands to emphasize the trifling nature of such concerns.

Love of his cousins and Elizabeth had prevented Darcy from taking just such action. To him, Anne was unwell, but never appeared to be upon death's door as her mother called it. A more mercenary man would marry one, wait for her to die, and then marry again, just to procure another estate. Taking another bow, Darcy's patience ended.

"Again I tell you, I shall see to my betrothed and her comfort after I have changed."

Darcy returned to the Master's chambers of Rosings and met with his man Simmons.

Allowing his valet to undress him, he awaited the water for a bath. He was not unfeeling towards Anne, she was his dear cousin. But he had only ever briefly intended to marry her once when the scheme was first pressed by all of his older relations. That fleeting reconciliation to a loveless marriage occurred while he mistakenly believed Elizabeth Bennet promised to another and before his other cousin, Colonel Richard Fitzwilliam, acquainted them to his secret love affair with Anne. His future companion had once described his life as a Shakespearean comedy, yet if matters did not change soon, Darcy would likely find him the hero of a tragedy.

"Sir, would you care to wear your charcoal coat or full black?" Simmons asked as another servant motioned Darcy's bath was prepared.

"Black." Darcy climbed into the tub and slunk into the hot water with his long legs bending up at the knee. If Anne's deterioration in fact existed, the perilous future of his family and personal happiness hung in the balance. Certainly, if Lady Catherine lost Rosings to a late, madness-induced will by her late husband, Sir Lewis de Bourgh, he was not prepared to take on the old baggage at Pemberley. This whole trouble began and ended with one man, Wickham. Had he simply disappeared, gone to America or elsewhere after Darcy paid him the value of the living willed to him by his own father, none of this would be happening. But Wickham ran off with Darcy's own sister, before her sixteenth birthday. The two now married, it would be nary impossible to avoid probate should Anne pass away unmarried. A bastard child, a will of a madman, and too much wealth for unscrupulous souls to manage, Darcy thought sourly.

After soaking for a full quarter hour, Darcy called Simmons for his clothes. His black suit of the finest cloth London could offer cut his tall frame into a handsome figure, but Darcy didn't need confidence in his appearance. The women of the Ton and even lower circles had ever chased after him as a fair prize to be caught. Yet it was one country miss who nearly died by his horse in a horrific accident last autumn that had captured his heart. Darcy wished he had managed to stop in London, if only to see his Elizabeth again.

"Shall I unpack your trunk, sir, or do you plan to travel again soon?" Simmons asked as he brushed small bits of lint off his master's coat.

Darcy tugged on this coat sleeve, glancing in the mirror, horrified at how gaunt his own face appeared. One year shy of his thirtieth birthday and yet the ghost of his father stared back at him in the lines and fatigue under his eyes.

"Please wait for my audience with Miss de Bourgh. At the very least we shall spend a week here so I may again go over the estate accounts." Despite wishing he could return to his love, and drag Richard out to Kent if necessary, Fitzwilliam Darcy couldn't keep avoiding his responsibilities forever.

Chapter Three

Sunlight poured through a dusty window at the top of the landing allowing Charlotte Collins a moment to check her disposition in the looking glass at the top of the servant's staircase before entering Anne de Bourgh's sick room. Her normally invigorating afternoon walk to Rosings was ruined by her husband's insistence on attending her, claiming concern over her earlier fatigue. She would have to remember to curtail her fibs when it came to her stamina in the middle of the day, though sidestepping Mr. Collins' regular attentions couldn't last.

With a cheery smile and her fake reading material in hand, Charlotte inhaled through her nose and stepped inside.

"Charlotte, you are early." The excitement in Anne's voice couldn't be mistaken, though it barely rose above a hoarse whisper.

"Shhh...no need to wear yourself out, Anne. My husband insisted upon walking with me, completely removing the time where I usually stroll your lovely gardens and park before attending to you . . ." Charlotte gave her friend an impertinent laugh, knowing Anne loved to hear about Charlotte's walks. In some ways, walking the gardens of Rosings reminded Charlotte of her life when it was more carefree in Hertfordshire, tromping after her friend, Elizabeth Bennet, in woods, streams, and fields.

Darcy appeared outside of his cousin's room moments later, shocked at the familiarity he heard between Anne and one that was unfamiliar, yet still comforting in an odd way. This shock kept him eavesdropping, as he stood rooted to the very floor and couldn't have performed a different action if he had tried.

"Did you harvest . . ." A fit of coughing prevented Anne's thought from completion. Charlotte quickly poured a glass of water for the lady to drink. As Anne lay back to rest from her coughing fit, Charlotte absently raked her fingers through the woman's thinning hair, sitting on the edge of her bed.

"Yes, the new crop finally came in and I expect to have more than enough for my plans."

"I'm so sorry you are unhappy. I cannot imagine my father forcing me to marry such a man."

Charlotte frowned for a moment, remembering the lack of aid her father gave in avoiding Mr. Collins' particular attention. Of course, Mr. Collins, due to inherit the Bennet home in Hertfordshire called Longbourn, was originally set to marry one of his cousins, and Charlotte's best friend. But Elizabeth Bennet had scorned Collins' proposal, and she had even warned Charlotte he was not a nice man. The chance of leaving her family home as a successful married woman, with a future of returning to her neighborhood on one distant day, had caused Charlotte to throw caution to the wind. She always thought happiness in marriage was a matter of chance, she just never thought herself to be so unlucky.

"It was not so much a forced marriage as the only offer ever made." Charlotte winced at the embarrassment of such a confession. "Perhaps marriages of convenience are less a savings and more a waste than we thought! Now shall we get back to Lady Helena and her dastardly Uncle seeking to steal her inheritance?" Both ladies laughed at the irony of their situations as

Charlotte pulled the contraband novel from the hiding space below Anne's bed.

The novelty of Anne's laugh startled Darcy back to the present. He entered the room and the young woman playing companion to his sickly wife halted him in his tracks. He remembered now, it was that odious parson's wife, the one who had taken the place of his dear Elizabeth at the altar. He pretended not to see Charlotte drop the book and slide it under the bed with a nudge of her slipper.

"Fitzwilliam!" Anne's gasp brought on another fit of coughs, and Charlotte and Darcy reached for the glass of water at the same time, spilling the clear liquid down the lace runner over the nightstand and into a wet puddle on the pale green rug.

"Blast!"

Anne's coughing continued.

"Pardon me, Mr. Darcy." Charlotte scrambled to right the glass, pour more water, and hand it to Anne who was now gulping her breaths between coughs.

"Ssh. Slowly, Anne. Don't fret, you will only feel worse."

Fitzwilliam Darcy stood at a complete loss. Anne's hair hung limply around her shoulders, her complexion the normal pale white he'd always seen. But the rattle in her cough and bluish tinge of her fingertips convinced him. The young girl he had chased and teased as a boy was slipping away from this world.

"Forgive me, I must write a letter. It is a pleasure to see you again, Mrs. Collins." Darcy bowed to the two women and strode confidently out of the suite, into the hall, and back towards his bedchamber, nearly knocking a squattish man, in possession of far too much forehead, to the ground.

Immediately, the man bowed in a deep bend, taking full responsibility for the offense.

"Mr. Darcy, may I say how pleased we are to hear of your return. It is a most celebrated event."

The gall of this man struck Darcy dumb. "I should hope my summons to Rosings is not an event to celebrate. My cousin is on her death bed."

"No, I mean to say, that is, it is most celebrated that you should return to Rosings, to wed, and as your presence brings an air of prestige that no other…"

Darcy pinched the bridge of his nose. He wanted nothing more than to return to his chamber and pen the missive he must to his other cousin, Colonel Fitzwilliam, hoping he could finally get away. Finally, the portly man's stuttering ended and Darcy realized he was waiting for his response. On what, he could not say as he had quit listening at "prestige."

"Certainly. Is there business I can help you with, Mr. . . ." Darcy purposely trailed off, not wishing to even utter the man's name. How this bumbling fool could have ever thought himself elevated enough for the likes of his Elizabeth, he did not know. But it was arrogance, and Darcy despised arrogance where no true superiority of the mind existed.

"Collins sir. Reverend Collins, at your most humble service, Mr. Darcy."

If this weren't indeed a grave situation, Darcy would think himself trapped in a play of comedy not of his own making. His cousin was dying, her mother couldn't be bothered, he might have no choice but to marry her to save the estate and risk losing his Elizabeth forever, and this pompous weasel was bowing to him. Again.

"Thank you, Mr. Collins." Darcy gave a pert nod of dismissal and tried to sidestep the man, to no avail.

"Mr. Darcy, might I offer my pastoral services in this extreme time of grief? I have served her Ladyship for a number of years now and in her great wisdom, she has encouraged my counseling efforts to be at the ready for any such situation as my flock may require. As parson, I pray most earnestly that you look to our Heavenly Father at this time of loss and rely on Scripture for your answers before hardening your heart."

"Mr. Collins, my cousin still breathes!" Darcy took back his thought of being caught in a comedy. This was a nightmare. "Good day, sir."

This time he physically brushed the sycophant aside. He was not two steps when the man dared to call after him.

"Pardon my intrusion, but perchance you've seen my wife, Charlotte, Mr. Darcy?"

Darcy wheeled around on the spot and narrowed his eyes at the man. "Your wife?"

Mr. Collins finally felt the disapproval he earned earlier and physically shrank an inch or two in stature under Darcy's glare. "Yes. Mrs. Collins. She reads sermons to Mrs. Darcy daily."

Realization struck Darcy immediately, and he did not wish for the kind Charlotte to be caught hiding a novel under a bed. He surmised the reality of Mrs. Collins' visits to his ailing cousin were unknown and as Darcy held not one ounce of respect for Mr. Collins, he would certainly preserve his cousin's privacy to her secrets and by proxy, her friend.

"Sermons. Of course. Yes, I did hear your wife reading to my cousin just moments ago.

Wait here and I shall inquire." Darcy once more walked past the man, his nostrils twitching at the overpowering smell of cheap cologne masking a failure to bathe.

"I shall accompany you and be of pastoral assistance." Mr. Collins took a few steps after Darcy, but froze when Mr. Darcy's much taller stature immediately turned back around to address him.

"You forget yourself, sir; perhaps my cousin is not decent for another man's visit. Do you make a habit of barging in on the sick rooms of every lady in your district?"

Mr. Collins face flushed to a deep shade of beet red. As he stammered more apologies, Darcy swiftly opened the bedroom door to Anne's sitting room to gain entrance to her bedchamber. He interrupted a rather rousing reading from Mrs. Collins on the topic of Lady Helena's near escape from her Uncle's estate by clearing his throat. Charlotte crimsoned and immediately hid the book behind her back.

"Forgive me, Anne. Mr. Collins is waiting in the hall for his wife."

Darcy didn't miss the fleeting look of disgust on Mrs. Collins face before she hastened to the bed to gently clasp Anne's hand in farewell.

Gently, Darcy pulled the novel from Mrs. Collins hands as it waggled behind her back in front of him. He bowed to Anne and saw Mrs. Collins to the sitting room.

"Mr. Darcy, about the reading material–"

"There's no need to explain, but after my earlier run-ins with Mr. Collins, perhaps it should remain with me? If it brings Anne a small amount of comfort, I shall offer to continue the story of Lady Helena and her dangerous adventures."

Charlotte nodded and flashed a brilliant smile. Suddenly, the bloom was gone from her face and she appeared stricken.

"Good day, Mr. Darcy. I'm sorry we met again under such sad circumstances and please tell Miss de Bourgh I shall see her tomorrow."

"Thank you, I believe my cousin would enjoy your presence."

Mrs. Collins opened the sitting room door to the hallway to find her husband pacing. She sighed and took his arm as he led her back down the grand staircase.

Darcy shook his head and returned to Anne's bedchamber, seizing the same chair previously occupied by Charlotte. He opened the book and began to read, watching with contentment as Anne smiled and relaxed against her pillows.

In a few minutes, her breathing regulated, though it was very shallow for his tastes. He gently kissed her hand to take his leave, and resolved to not let anything or anyone get in the way of the letter he must write. He could not handle this alone.

Chapter Four

Hyde Park blossomed around Elizabeth Bennet as the early floral armies of spring marched forward, brashly breaking the earth around them. Attended by a maid employed by the Gardiner household named Anna, Elizabeth was dismayed that the warmer weather and start of the London Season brought more patrons to the park.

Standing before a gigantic shrub carved into the shape of an elephant, Elizabeth stopped walking and giggled.

"Miss?" Anna, who had been conspicuously walking behind her charge, lost the short distance between them when Miss Bennet abruptly stopped.

"Sorry, Anna. I was merely remembering the first time Mr. Darcy and I walked these gardens. He makes a most impressive elephant," Elizabeth explained.

"Yes, miss." Anna demurely nodded and continued walking after her employer's niece. Twice daily walks were an exercise the other maids eschewed, but Anna did not mind Miss Elizabeth's jolly spirit and energies. It certainly was more pleasurable to exercise than it was to scrub chamber pots.

On their second circuit, Elizabeth spied a handsome fellow wearing the robin's breast red coat of His Majesty's Army. The tall, stocky fellow with reddish-brown sideburns nodded to her and touched the brim of his cap. It was the sign Elizabeth looked for every day. It meant the man, Colonel Richard Fitzwilliam, had news, and would be along shortly to call upon her at her relations' home in Cheapside.

"Come, Anna, we must hurry home." Elizabeth slightly lifted her skirts to walk briskly towards her uncle's carriage, with poor Anna nearly needing to run to keep up. But the joy was positively too overwhelming for Elizabeth to keep under good regulation. Perhaps Richard had a letter from her Fitzwilliam? Perhaps he at last had leave and could go to Kent to free her fiancée from this scheme of theirs to play the family false.

Breathless, Anna managed a return to the carriage long after Elizabeth had entered and settled herself. Catching back her calm, the maid, who was a few years older than Miss Bennet, gazed sternly at the woman whose love life had caused such uproar in the household.

"Miss Bennet, you frightened me that you would have left me behind. I did not know ladies could dart so in public."

Elizabeth left her vigil of the window to watch the Colonel's progress to his own horse to smile broadly at the maid. Anna's kindness and care had nearly transformed her into a personal maid of sorts, and Elizabeth would genuinely miss her constant companion when her new life with Mr. Darcy began. "No one knows me here, I can afford a bit of reckless abandon now and again."

Absent-mindedly, Elizabeth flexed her left foot, the very ankle she broke last autumn diving out the way of Mr. Darcy's horse, Alexander. "Besides, I still so desperately cherish my abilities to walk and ramble. Trust me, once you lose your ability to walk, even for a short time, you remind yourself to not take your health for granted again!"

The maid nodded sagely as the Gardiner carriage gave a lurch and stopped only to lurch again to turn onto the main road connecting Mayfair and Cheapside. The Colonel's horse followed the carriage in a lazy, disinterested manner and Richard was careful to take a number of detours to disguise his destination. As he led his horse Sampson down a less-traveled alleyway to round the block, the stench of London's daily life assaulted his senses. Careful to remain in the middle as much as possible, Richard hoped he was not mucking with the beast's natural sense of direction with all of these obscured routes.

Two ladies with extravagant costumes, just a touch too fashionable for the hour, strolled the path of Hyde Park with a nanny and babe behind them. One wore a dark blue gown in an attempt to hide her body's changes from recently giving birth. The other wore a garish gown made of a gold and orange Indian sari, with matching plumage in her hair.

"I was correct, I told you it was that upstart Elizabeth Bennet talking about Mr. Darcy! Louisa, we must call on Darcy House this very afternoon." Caroline Bingley whispered hoarsely to her sister.

"Curious, I believe that was his cousin who left around the same time. Perhaps it is he who is interested in Eliza. We both know the Bennets love their red coats." Louisa Hurst gave a laugh that most carefully sounded like a snark.

So angry to see her adversary, in London, with connections of some kind to Mr. Darcy, the feathers in Caroline's head bobbled furiously from the shudder of her clenched jaw. Narrowing her eyes to see the last of the carriage rolling away towards the less fashionable side of town, incidentally the same direction of the Hurst town home though that home was not so far as to be labeled as Cheapside, Caroline stomped her slippered foot in exasperation. Too many times Darcy had slipped through her fingers, and Caroline was determined to not let it happen again.

"I feel a headache coming on." Louisa touched her forehead for effect.

"You always feel a headache coming on. I want to call on Miss Darcy, forgive me, Mrs. Wickham, as soon as we are able."

Louisa frowned at her sister and with a swish of her skirts, began walking towards her own equipage. "Allow the poor woman to return to London, if you please. I have no interest in running to our brother in Bath."

Caroline pulled a fan from her reticule and snapped it open to cover her expression of utter disgust should they pass a lady of importance on their departure. She had not been taken on

Charles' wedding trip with Jane, a manipulation she instigated, as an attempt to ensnare Darcy at Netherfield Park after Charles' departure. Instead, she had missed the opportunity to ingratiate herself further with Darcy's younger sister who was coincidentally in the same town enjoying her wedding trip. The world was patently unfair and Caroline refused to think for one moment if she only ceased trying to dictate her own fate, perhaps Providence might shine more favorably upon her.

Chapter Five

The Gardiner town home at Twenty-Seven Gracechurch Street in Cheapside was aflutter with activity. Elizabeth and her maid Anna entered the home to hear Mrs. Gardiner speaking excitedly from the sitting room. A deep baritone voice, unfamiliar to Elizabeth, and certainly not belonging to her uncle, could also be heard. Elizabeth looked to Anna as the maid assisted in removing her cloak and bonnet.

Elizabeth paused for a moment to check her appearance in the peering glass mounted in the hallway. If her aunt was to introduce her to a new acquaintance, she wished to look her best. Elizabeth Bennet had never been a vain creature. However, since her secret alliance with

Mr. Fitzwilliam Darcy of Derbyshire, the young woman of little consequence from Hertfordshire took greater care in how she was to be perceived by others.

"I am utterly conflicted, I love both paper patterns equally it seems. The olive and cream stripes are very calm and soothing, while this navy blue with a touch of gold might appeal more to Mr. Gardiner, I believe." Madeleine Gardiner held up the two samples of wallpaper against the aging roses currently in her plastered in her sitting room.

"Observing this room receives a fair amount of sun, might I suggest the olive and cream paper might hold up better to nature's assault from these gorgeous windows you possess?" the mysterious man suggested.

"Are we to redecorate the sitting room as well?" Elizabeth raised an eyebrow as she cheekily spoke out to announce her arrival. Her aunt made the necessary introductions, explaining to Elizabeth the man was no other than Mr. Thaddeus Warren, an up-and-coming interior decorator who came highly recommended from Mrs. Henrietta Carlton, the dressmaker.

Elizabeth took a look at both wallpaper samples and had to admit that she agreed with the decorator. The navy blue, a heavily masculine color scheme, would not serve as a decoration she would find herself enjoying in a room with it plastered on the walls.

"I suspect we have company soon to arrive, would it be acceptable if I use Uncle's study?"

Madeleine Gardner waved her hand at her niece and agreed, knowing without asking who the impending visitor was likely to be. The cousin of Mr. Fitzwilliam Darcy, Colonel Richard Fitzwilliam, had enjoyed a number of dinners and evenings in her home. If Lizzie were not so in love with the dark man from Derbyshire, Mrs. Gardiner began to think the jovial natures of her niece and the Colonel would easily suit one another.

"Have Anna attend you, and the post is on your uncle's desk. I believe I spied a letter for you." Mrs. Gardiner smiled as Elizabeth bowed her head to the decorator out of courtesy, and then nearly leapt from the room.

The pile of correspondence on the desk included a number of letters addressed to her Uncle Edward, but at last, Lizzie found a strange missive from Kent. It was not from her Mr. Darcy, but instead from her dearest friend from Hertfordshire, Charlotte Lucas, now a married woman to her cousin Collins.

Dearest Lizzie,

A Virtue of Marriage

Spring approaches in our lovely corner of the kingdom and I found myself wishing to invite you for a visit at your earliest convenience. My father and Maria were to come for the Easter holidays, but a change in their plans opens an opportunity for us to reunite sooner, if it pleases you.

You promised to come see me once settled, and I am happy to report the parsonage so generously bestowed by Lady Catherine has at last become home. It would ever so delight my husband and your cousin, to have you visit and partake in the scenic grounds of the Lady Catherine's estate. There are many paths for walking, and you would most certainly enjoy our regular inclusions at dinners with Lady Catherine herself. Please say you shall come. I eagerly await your reply.

Your Longtime Friend,

Charlotte Collins

Elizabeth's hands trembled as she read, reread and then read once more, the missive. She bit her lower lip to keep from shouting out at the wonderful news of receiving an invitation to Kent, to the very estate where Fitzwilliam was kept prisoner. This whole business of arranged and unarranged marriages did not suit her at all, and though in her heart and mind she trusted Fitzwilliam to prevail, the stabs and pangs of jealousy never truly dissipated while he was away.

The sounds of the Colonel's precipitous arrival startled Elizabeth back to the present matters at hand and she swiftly refolded Charlotte's letter to tuck into her dress pocket. She smiled in preparation for the man to enter the study and glanced over to Anna, sitting calmly in the far corner of the room. Giving the maid a wink, the two shared a silent laugh as Richard entered the room.

"Miss Bennet, may I say how lovely you look today." The dashing Colonel bowed low to his favorite cousin's intended.

"Colonel, you are so flattering, but I do think we might dispense with pleasant formalities. You have news?" Elizabeth's throat clenched as her heart hoped Richard held a letter from her Fitzwilliam.

"I've had a letter from Darcy."

Jubilation bubbled over in Elizabeth heart, and she finally felt she could breathe easily. "Has he written to me?"

The Colonel shook his head, and Elizabeth's hopes crashed to the ground. "I see." She took a seat in her favorite chair next to the bookcases in Uncle's study. The Colonel looked around him and found the wooden chair beside Mr. Gardiner's desk as a suitable place to rest.

"The situation in Kent has become desperate. I am to leave tomorrow, as I have finally secured permission for leave from the Major General. I only wished to visit here so that I might keep you abreast of the latest developments. Darcy writes that our cousin, Anne, is . . ." The man trailed off as his emotions began to overwhelm him.

Elizabeth witnessed the difficulties her visitor experienced in saying the words she could easily guess. "Your presence is needed at once," she said softly.

Richard nodded. "I shall leave for Kent in the morning on horseback."

Elizabeth pursed her lips and worked out her plan in her head. Charlotte had invited her to visit at her earliest convenience. And here was an opportunity to not only travel with a maid, as she was sure her aunt and uncle would insist upon, but with a member of His Majesty's Finest. Would Fitzwilliam be angry for her to leave London without his knowledge? But that thought flittered away as Elizabeth smiled at the opportunity to surprise Fitzwilliam as he had surprised her these last two months with his unannounced returns to the city.

"Colonel, would you consider assisting me in a surprise attack on your cousin and travel to Kent not on horseback, but by carriage?"

A consummate prankster himself, Richard at first felt keen to aid Miss Bennet, but visions of his aunt's wrath made him question the wisdom of such a plan. "While I would love nothing more than to please my cousin with aiding your travel, I hesitate that your presence might complicate our plans . . ."

Wrinkling her nose, Elizabeth shook her head and retrieved the letter from her pocket. "Oh, I would never presume to stay at Rosings uninvited. It is that I have just today received an invitation to visit my dear friend Charlotte and her husband, my cousin."

"The very same cousin you refused to marry?" The Colonel asked, forgetting that was a confidence Darcy had shared. "Forgive me, I spoke out of turn."

Steadying her emotions with a deep breath through her nose, Elizabeth managed to keep her composure that Richard should know of her past. "Fear not, I am not surprised Fitzwilliam made you aware of the particulars. You are trustee to my future safety. But yes, the very same man, though I do not think now that he is married he should behave untoward in my direction."

Richard agreed with Elizabeth with a slow nod of his head, finally considering her proposed travel arrangements more carefully. After the gossip in the newspaper, bringing Elizabeth Bennet to Kent might prove to be the perfect distraction to keep Lady Catherine off his and Darcy's true aims. And with Richard there, his aunt would never succeed in forcing a sudden marriage between Darcy and Anne. He looked again at his cousin's intended and measured her mettle as she sat there, fire in her eyes, chin jutted out. This lady was a warrior; there was no doubt about it. Richard would be a fool to dismiss her offer of aid, even if it did make her the sacrificial lamb in the plan.

"Miss Bennet, you are a crafty one, I shall warrant you that much. I hope my cousin knows what it is he has found in you." The compliment was met with a tinkling laughter that made the Colonel join with his deeper bass. "I accept your plan and shall return this evening to discuss the particulars with your uncle."

"I shall prepare him for your visit, sir." Elizabeth rose from her chair to see the colonel out and smiled as he left at nearly the same time as Mr. Warren. Both Mrs. Gardiner and Elizabeth stood in the entryway for a moment and her aunt asked Lizzie for the news.

"I am to leave for Kent in the morning, Aunt Maddie, and rescue my knight!" Elizabeth laughed as she pecked her aunt on the cheek and hurried up the stairs. She had much to pack, and little time to prepare.

Chapter Six

Regular post amused Mr. Bennet of Hertfordshire. Since losing his favorite daughter to her stubborn will, the letters from his brother-in-law Gardiner rarely interested him beyond a glance. The latest letter, though, appeared to have significant heft to it as it sat, carefully folded upon his desk.

"Mr. Bennet! Mr. Bennet! Come quickly, a carriage has been spotted!"

Robert Bennet cast his eyes to his easily excitable wife standing in the doorway to his study. Francine Bennet had not ceased to speak about the impending arrival of their eldest daughter, now fashioned as Mrs. Charles Bingley, since breakfast. She now stood waving her familiar object of comfort, a lace handkerchief, beckoning her husband to leave his den of refuge.

"Mrs. Bennet, until the carriage has arrived and Mr. and Mrs. Bingley have been welcomed into our home, kindly allow me some peace."

"You have no compassion, sir 'tis a momentous day for any mother to welcome home a married daughter. A momentous day indeed!"

Despite her chastisement, Mrs. Bennet did manage to leave her husband alone to await the carriages arrival. Mr. Bennet poured himself a drink and considered the unopened letter from London. If the letter should prove upsetting, the visit of his most obedient and serene daughter, Jane, may alleviate any ill effects. Should the letter not prove upsetting, well, that was an unlikelihood Robert would not deign to expect.

Slicing the seal of the letter, a number of papers were folded with only the top letter in his brother's hand.

Brother Bennet,

Although your continued silence from the numerous updates I have sent regarding your daughter Elizabeth leads me to believe you are uninterested in her future, the father in me refuses to give up the hope that a reconciliation might still come to pass. My last letter explained my reservations concerning a suitor for Elizabeth's hand, a Mr. Fitzwilliam Darcy of Derbyshire.

I've had it confirmed through my sister Phillips that the man is indeed the same who nearly killed my niece with his reckless horseback riding. As the injuries to Elizabeth are not lasting, and she appears in fine health, I'm confident the accident has forged a rather strong bond between the two young people.

Mr. Darcy began to call on my family a number of times each week, by direct result, I am told, of Elizabeth visiting his town home without invitation to return a book lent to her during her lengthy recuperation at Netherfield Park. I did my best to dissuade the man from his interests in Elizabeth because I feared with such wealth, a man was unlikely to be honorable with his intentions.

While I cannot in clear conscience say I was incorrect, as Mr. Darcy's family has intervened to make him marry his sickly cousin in Kent, your daughter considers herself engaged to the man. And despite his difficulties in managing his family's expectations, Mr. Darcy has settled an extensive trust upon your unmarried daughter with his cousin and myself as trustees.

Robert Bennet's heart clenched in his chest. How could his brother Gardiner be such an imbecile to not recognize a rich man providing for his mistress? If Mr. Darcy had such designs of marriage towards his Lizzie, there had been ample time for the man to come honorably to Longbourn and discuss such matters with her father. The very fact that this rich man had waited until his daughter was unprotected, in London, proved to Mr. Bennet no such wedding should ever occur between his favorite daughter and Mr. Bingley's closest friend.

Lizzie has accepted the invitation of her friend, Mrs. Charlotte Collins, and recently left our home to go to Kent. I am apprehensive about her reception to the very estate where Mr. Darcy is expected to wed his cousin, but both my wife and niece dismissed my concerns. We both know Lizzie's will is ironclad where her heart is concerned, and I felt I had no choice but to assist her in her aims.

I pray these young people, including Mr. Darcy's cousin, know their business as their intentions are to switch Mr. Darcy as groom to their cousin, a Miss Anne de Bourgh, with the man traveling to Kent with Elizabeth, a Colonel Richard Fitzwilliam. I admire their pluck for the Colonel's parents, the Earl and Countess of Matlock, and Miss de Bourgh's mother, Lady Catherine de Bourgh, are opposed.

Raised voices outside of his study alerted Mr. Bennet that it was likely the Bingleys had arrived. He frowned as he remembered the meddling nature of the woman when described by his buffoon of a cousin, William Collins, as his esteemed patroness. Even if such a scheme were truly intended by these rich men with Elizabeth in their clutches, there was no chance such a woman would allow her daughter to marry a Colonel instead of one of the wealthiest landowners in all of England. When had his bright and charming daughter become such an idiot to not see these men wished to play her false?

Should Lizzie triumph; our families shall see ourselves aligned with no less than an Earl and his family, a development I believe my sister would most relish. This is why I beg of you to consider reconciliation with your daughter in the interest of family harmony. And should Lizzie fail, the consequences of such an effort will ruin her place in society and she shall need the love and support of her relatives to survive. She will have plenty of resources should she lose her Mr. Darcy, the gentleman did mitigate that risk, but you and I both know Elizabeth Bennet could never live the life of an outcast.

Your servant,

Edward Gardiner

Inhaling sharply through his nose, Robert Bennet did not even look at the enclosed papers detailing a whore's settlement upon his daughter. He crumpled every shred of parchment from London and stood up from his desk to toss the offending missive into the flames. In the back of his mind, he had considered inviting Lizzie home once the Bingleys were settled back into the neighborhood and his wife's anger dissipated. His own anger over her disobedience when he had wished nothing more than to never lose her as he nearly had when Mr. Darcy ran her over with that piece to his left his heart less than a month after she ran the London.

Tears welled in the eyes of the sixth heir of the Longbourn estate as he leaned against the mantle and observed the flames devouring the papers. With the futures of three more daughters to secure because of the blasted entail, his Lizzie's folly was too much. He used the poker to adjust the embers of the letter so that no scrap remained unburned. As his brother-in-law's request reduced to ashes, one truth remained. Elizabeth Bennet was little better than dead to her family.

Chapter Seven

Georgiana Wickham flounced down the stairs at Darcy House in Grosvenor Square at a perfect mid-morning arousal for the lady of the house. Checking her porcelain complexion in the mirror in a hall outside of the breakfast room, she entered to dine with the brightest disposition a nearly 16-year-old bride without a care in the world could possess.

As she filled a plate with her favorite pastries, her smile dampened a bit as her rascally handsome husband refused to acknowledge her presence with even so much as a glance up from his paper, let alone the gentlemanly custom of rising for a lady entering the room. Puckering her lips into a slight pout, she popped a small

A Virtue of Marriage

strawberry into her mouth and spun around to face the table.

"If you eat nothing but sweets, your waistline will grow to unimaginable proportions." George Wickham still refused to look up from the London paper, scanning furtively for any news of Darcy's marriage to Anne de Bourgh.

Georgiana's slight pout became a full on lip quibble at the harsh tones from her husband. Only married a little less than half a year, she already noticed he lessened the frequency in which he visited her chambers, preferring instead to stay out at all hours. "Does my body displease you? Is this why you no longer come to me?"

George Wickham let out a frustrated sigh and shuffled the newspaper closed before tossing it down the table in dismissal. He waited for a servant to refill his coffee and took a sip of the piping hot liquid, mindful not to scorch his mouth. With a clatter, he set the cup down, sloshing a small amount of the dark beverage onto the pristine white tablecloth underneath. Ignoring his faux pas, he tossed his napkin onto his plate full of half eaten food.

"Of course not, Georgie. I am just so bloody bored being cooped up in this house. Why don't we go out tonight, just you and I, and enjoy the theater? Must we stay cooped up in this town home for the entire Season?"

"Brother said we must stay out of society. That once we return from Bath we may use the town home until he returns." Georgiana picked up a new pastry, then thought better of it and placed it back down on her plate. She reached for her tea instead.

"Mrs. Wickham," he said slyly, waiting for her to smile at her fresh moniker, "you as a married woman must not always do as your brother says. As madame of the house, you may set the social calendar at your whim."

Georgiana looked thoughtfully at the window that overlooked a small garden in front of the home, walled off from the busy street. Aside from visits to her modiste, she had not ventured out much from the house as her brother had instructed. Last autumn, he had made it clear that unless she behave accordingly, her dowry and allowance would be kept from them. But surely one night, while he was away in Kent, wouldn't cause any harm. Then again, the anger in her brother's eyes before she married made her pause. What if he did cut her and George off?

She shook her head. "No, Brother has enough to deal with in soon losing our cousin and being forced to marry. We must not add to his burdens."

"Yes, poor Anne is not long for this life I'm afraid. But, as you know, when your brother returns, we shall have to go into full mourning at least for a small amount of time. Surely, she would wish for us to enjoy Town as much as we can before that unhappy event. Anne has the kindest heart a soul could ask for." George turned on the charm and waited. He reached out to touch his wife's hand and knew he had won his argument the second her face turned to look at his with a softened expression.

"It is a distance to Kent, and Fitzwilliam might never know. I would like to see the new comedy being performed."

"The Imposter?" Wickham smirked, surprised his little wife was aware of the title.

Georgiana blushed and nodded. "Fitzwilliam had me read it last year upon turning fifteen and I have always wanted to see it performed live."

Wickham picked up her hand properly and bestowed a kiss upon it. "Then tonight, let us shed this melancholy we both feel and will be served more of in the very near future and take a night for French debauchery!"

Georgiana giggled at the overly dramatic nature of her husband.

"On the stage only, of course," he added with another sly grin.

"I'll go now and select an appropriate gown." Georgiana rose from the table, this time with her husband offering her the proper behavior due a lady by rising with her.

"And I shall go to find a trinket for you, though it will hardly be worth a glance when the jewel of the Darcy family dons my arm this evening."

George gave his wife a flourished bow, making her giggle more, and waited until he could hear her running up the stairs before collapsing back into the chair and rubbing his forehead. Nothing rested heavier on a man than a severe lack of both funds and the freedom to garner more.

No, his plan to elope with Georgiana crumbled when upon discovery and the deed done on paper and in the bedroom, Darcy produced the full will of the late George Darcy. Should Georgiana marry before the age of majority and without the consent of her guardians, the full dowry would remain under Darcy's control until she should reach majority age and then transfer to her husband. With Georgiana's sixteenth birthday being in three short weeks, Wickham had a five-year sentence to play out before he controlled a pence of the thirty thousand pounds.

Rising to leave the breakfast room and enter Darcy's study, Wickham helped himself to a healthy portion of the finest port and looked again at the business papers he had pulled out and placed on the grand desk. Hopefully, with enough details of the deals Darcy had with the gentry under his belt he would be able to forge an acquaintance with one or more of the men listed on the papers. A very lucrative acquaintance.

Chapter Eight

Elizabeth Bennet gently lifted the hem of her skirt and eyed the two flights of worn stone steps before her. The stair cases marked the entrance to Rosings, the estate owned by Mr. Darcy's aunt, Lady Catherine de Bourgh, an entrance that stared her down with its dark medieval decor. There certainly were scores upon scores of windows, just as her cousin Collins had described last autumn when he bragged about his patroness. But each pane of glass appeared as the narrowed eyes of a great mythological beast with the ornate stone decorations and a number of ghastly-sculpted gargoyles on each parapet.

"Perhaps I ought simply take the carriage to the parsonage? I don't wish to impose upon your aunt." Elizabeth looked to her right towards Colonel Fitzwilliam. She strained to keep up with his pace as his longer legs and experience with the uneven steps gave him much advantage.

The Colonel laughed and offered his arm to assist Miss Bennet the rest of the way. "And miss the look of surprise on Darcy's face? Never! Besides, the parsonage is unlikely to have resources for the horses. Darcy makes sure my aunt's stables are well staffed. Give the horses their rest." The last inn stop they skipped entirely on account of their excitement to see their future spouses.

An empty dread filled Elizabeth's stomach as the monstrous green lacquered doors opened to allow them entry. The Colonel greeted the longtime butler of the home, but Elizabeth's attentions were arrested at the site of Mr. Darcy approaching the entryway with such a somber expression it broke her heart.

The dark brown eyes of Fitzwilliam Darcy blinked numerous times, as he was most certain they must have been deceiving him. There stood Richard with none other than his beloved Elizabeth, the woman who haunted his dreams and filled his heart, yet though he was bursting to dash forward and greet her properly, he could not. Using years of practiced manners, the Master of Pemberley strolled forward in even measured steps. He gave a low bow to both of the new visitors.

"That's it?" The Colonel stepped forward to clap Darcy on the shoulder. "I travel lo these many miles from London with a particular companion and that formal bow is all the greeting we receive? Well, if I was a lady I should say –"

"Colonel, would you be so kind as to introduce me to your cousin? You spoke so much about him on our way from London." Elizabeth Bennett's voice rang clear as she looked pointedly towards the Butler and footmen observing their small party.

"Yes, Richard. Where are your manners?" Darcy risked a flash of a smile in Elizabeth's direction and it was all the reassurance she needed. She had no delusions coming to Kent even at the invitation of a friend was dangerous business.

"May I introduce Miss Elizabeth Bennet, an acquaintance from London who was coincidentally invited to visit her cousin and his wife at the parsonage? I offered her uncle to personally escort Miss Bennet seeing as I was traveling to the exact same location. Miss Bennet, this is my boring, droll cousin, Fitzwilliam Darcy. He owns property." The barbs of Richard Fitzwilliam did nothing to distract the young couple now formally introduced to play their farce.

"Miss Bennet, may I say it is a pleasure to meet you." Darcy gallantly offered for her hand and bent down to kiss it properly. Elizabeth let out a small sigh that only those closest to her could hear.

"FITZWILLIAM! Why are you carrying on so long in the hall?" Lady Catherine's booming voice echoed in the large expansive entryway.

The Colonel offered his arm to Elizabeth once more, aggravating Darcy, but playing his role. "Come, we must not leave my aunt waiting." The three entered the parlor to the sharp glare from the lady of the house. The unfamiliar young woman on her nephew's arm made Lady Catherine frown in disproval.

"Richard, whoever did you bring with you? I was not aware you were to bring a visitor, and a young woman at that, this is most unsuitable Come here, girl, let me see you properly."

Elizabeth's shoulders involuntarily pushed back at the older woman's verbal assault, but she felt Richard lightly nudge her where their arms connected as a sign to keep quiet.

"Aunt, a close acquaintance of mine had a niece traveling to visit your parson and his wife.

It seemed only gentlemanly that I escort Miss Bennet as I was headed the same."

"Miss Bennet? A Miss Bennet? Surely not that bit of muslin listed as your mistress Darcy! Yes, yes I've heard of her, she is to leave, at once! Hawkins! Hawkins!" Lady Catherine rose from her ornate chair to pull the cord hanging in the far corner of the room. The butler obediently appeared in the parlor. "Hawkins, escort this garbage out of my home this instant!" She pointed towards Elizabeth, whose mouth dropped in fear.

"Hawkins, if you wish to remain employed, you will not touch Miss Bennet." The cool, calm voice of Mr. Darcy negated his aunt's bluster.

"This is not your place, Fitzwilliam. How dare you have your cousin bring your mistress while your future wife lay dying above stairs? How dare you bring the same shame as my husband?"

Darcy continued to stand stoically, his arms clasped behind his back, just next to Elizabeth. If she inhaled deeply, she could smell his musk she knew all too well from their many walks in Hyde Park and elsewhere before this awful woman dragged him to Kent. The situation could not possibly be worse than she had imagined, but she had not truly expected a lady of the peerage to be so utterly without manners.

"Lady Catherine is mistaken, Hawkins. Miss Bennet is not here in any capacity related to me. She is here to visit her relations and no more. Is that clear?" Darcy's voice proved scarier to the poor butler than Lady Catherine's as the servant nodded and backed out of the room. Louis Hawkins had not recently been hired on at the estate, and though Lady Catherine indeed owned the home, it was not she who ruled the purse strings.

Lady Catherine looked to the three young people in her parlor and gave a sickening grin as Elizabeth looked to both men for what to do next. "It's clear now. The two of you share her favors, yes, that's it. I've heard of such things, in those dark circles of society, women who cater to particular tastes . . ."

"Close your mouth madame or I assure you I shall shut it for you!" The lion of Richard Fitzwilliam roared to life, releasing Elizabeth's arm as he marched forward to advance on his aunt. "That tongue of yours has always caused trouble in this family, and where my father might tolerate it, I shall not allow you to blacken my character, nor Darcy's, nor that of Miss Bennet. Am I clear?"

Lady Catherine de Bourgh suddenly shrank in stature at the dual assault from both of her nephews. Neither had ever spoken to her is such a manner and in her own home! But Lady Catherine was not an imbecile. There was no doubt this new madness in both of her nephews stemmed from this upstart before her, but her claws were in much too deep. No, to save her nephews, Lady Catherine would need to crafty. Cunning.

"You would speak to an old woman, your superior in such a way? Why I ought to have you whipped, boy! You are not welcome in this home, and I am most displeased you have not the manners to announce your travel companions. I am retiring to my rooms for the afternoon and I expect you both at dinner with your manners properly restored. Take this person to the parsonage if that is truly where she is destined for, but she is not for my company and that is final."

Lady Catherine pulled on the cord three times and a young footman appeared to escort her upstairs. Dramatically leaning on her cane, and the boy's arm, Lady Catherine left the room and for the first time in many minutes, Elizabeth Bennet felt enough relief to release the breath she had been holding.

Richard left the parlor not long after his aunt, closing the doors behind him, presumably to see to his Anne. Darcy led Elizabeth to the nearest sofa and she happily settled onto it.

"Fitzwilliam I am so sorry, truly sorry. I was a fool for letting Richard talk me into coming to the main house first. Such a fool!"

Darcy traced the jawline of his beloved with his finger and crooked her face up towards his. Kissing her with the passion of a man on the precipice of disaster, he pulled her upper body into a crush against his own with a tight embrace. Fearing discovery, he reluctantly released her to appear as indifferent acquaintances should his aunt send a servant.

"It is I who am sorry you heard those filthy words spew from my aunt. She is unbearable at best, but today she was—"

"She is losing her only daughter. I've seen people behave most oddly in the face of great tragedy and stress." Elizabeth gave her future husband a look of pure compassion. This was the same explanation she used to comfort herself when her memories of the night she was thrown out from her family home. It was the only explanation she could give for why her father would allow her mother to have behaved so abominably.

"That is no excuse. No excuse at all. She hardly ever sees her daughter, and . . . and I am rambling on when I have no inclination to speak to you about my aunt."

Elizabeth offered him a shy smile. She had not wanted to say as such, but her Mr. Darcy was quite clever in remembering their privacy was limited. She had not traveled for a day in a rambling carriage to talk about unpleasant matters.

"Are you pleased I came? I did think for a moment such a plan was—"

Darcy silenced her with another kiss. The delicious warmth she felt each time he placed his lips on her own made Elizabeth tingle down to her toes. Wishing to convey such joy, she nuzzled her nose on his own larger aristocratic profile, eliciting a rare laugh from him.

"I am overjoyed you are near. I have worried senselessly since leaving London. The situation here has become most dire." The serious tone behind his words added additional weight to Elizabeth's shoulders.

"And you have had no one to stand by you as you face it," she declared.

The simplicity of her statement resonated deep within Darcy's soul. No other woman had ever considered his feelings beyond passing fancies of his favorite drink or play or book so as to further discussion in a ballroom. He would have embraced her again had the doors to the parlor not opened once more, with Richard strolling in, clearly agitated.

"She is in a worse state than I ever imagined." The army man wasted no time in walking across the parlor to the small sideboard where his aunt kept spirits. Wisely pulling the decanter from the back, Richard poured the scotch that was not watered down to save money.

"I sent for you directly. That was the purpose of my express. I am only glad you finally secured leave," Darcy said.

"Has the doctor—"

Elizabeth cleared her throat, attracting the attention of both men. Meekly, she smiled and rubbed her hands over the lap of her dress. The discussion of another woman's health, one that was still a stranger made her uncomfortable. "I'm terribly sorry, but the Collinses are expecting me. Would one of you escort me to the parsonage with the carriage?" She looked directly at Darcy when she said the words.

"We should both go." Richard announced, downing his shot. "If we truly do not wish to raise talk, it's imperative the staff not see the two of you alone as much as possible. Aunt Catherine will be suspicious this entire visit, thanks to my damn need to play a prank."

Darcy helped Elizabeth up from the sofa, biting back his words that he agreed with his cousin's sentiment. Perhaps if they had not arrived together, and instead Elizabeth had been introduced to his aunt as a visitor to the parsonage . . . but it was too late to change his aunt's perceptions now.

"I shall call on you tomorrow. Do you plan to take your daily walk in the morning?" Darcy asked, most earnestly.

"Sir, unless you decide to break my other ankle by running me down with your horse, I believe it is safe to say I shall walk each morning the weather is fine." The two locked eyes and enjoyed another brief moment of connection until Richard cleared his throat.

"We'd better find a way to marry me and Anne quickly, the two of you won't last a week at this rate."

Chapter Nine

Arriving just before dinner, Elizabeth's presence in the county stood as a complete surprise to her cousin Mr. Collins. Both gentlemen from the main house escorted her; there was little rudeness he could offer. Charlotte, on the other hand, brightened at the sudden arrival of her friend she had only invited to visit last week when her father and sister had cut their own visit short.

Unfortunately, once inside the smaller cottage, the two nephews of Mr. Collins' esteemed patroness had to leave much too soon for Elizabeth's taste. With no opportunity to privately farewell, Elizabeth settled for a smoldering look from her intended and a joke from the Colonel about his dinner plans interfering with his digestion.

"I can assure you, Colonel, the meals at Rosings are very fine indeed! Why Mrs. Collins and I enjoyed Lady Catherine's invitation just last week, and the roast duck was superb. I only wish you had been present, Mr. Darcy, and you would agree that no finer a meal had been set." Mr. Collins bumbled on and on as the two men tried to leave for the third time in as many minutes.

"Mr. Collins, I believe Lady Catherine is waiting for her nephews to return. Thank you gentlemen for seeing to my friend's safe travels." Charlotte nodded her head as the men acknowledged her gratitude and appreciated her herding them towards the door, away from her husband.

Mr. Collins followed his wife and Elizabeth remained behind, breathing slowly until the door closed with a dull finality.

"How could you invite that woman to our home? You know Lady Catherine has an extreme dislike for my cousin after she shamelessly threw herself at Mr. Darcy in Hertfordshire and then again in London, from what I'm told!" Mr. Collins grabbed Charlotte's arm and shoved her violently into the parlor.

Charlotte did not cry out or say anything in response, and if Elizabeth had been ignorant of the parson's true nature, she might have been utterly shocked. Instead, she bore witness to her worst fears. Mr. Collins was not only a bully to her, as a result of her headstrong ways, but to all women, including his wife. Charlotte's disposition was as sweet and serene as Jane's; there could be no discord as a result of behavior on her part.

Elizabeth stepped forward, blocking Mr. Collins from further hurting his wife. "I am so thankful for your hospitality Mr. Collins. You are truly kind to invite me for the Easter holiday."

"No, Lizzie, you mustn't," Charlotte said.

"I know my business, Charlotte. My cousin and I have a long acquaintance with each other, afforded by our doomed courtship. But I am certain a man of the church could not possibly hold a grudge." Elizabeth narrowed her eyes at her cousin. She could not yet declare herself under Mr. Darcy's protection, but that did not change the unequivocal knowledge she held such protection. And this time, this time she was not going to go quietly to keep up appearances.

"You forget yourself, Cousin."

"Test me, Cousin," she emphasized the moniker, "Try my patience and see who my friends are." Elizabeth jutted out her chin as if to dare the man to strike her.

William Collins stood taller, adding a slight addition to his height, but Elizabeth Bennet did not flinch. What did she mean about her friends? She had traveled friendless to Kent, no doubt tossed from her aunt and uncle's for her poor behavior. He sniffed and looked beyond her to his wife, cowering behind. There was little he could do tonight to remove this harridan from his home, and he couldn't be bothered with such nuisances.

"I will take my dinner in my study. See to your friend's lodgings. Do not disturb my peace." He enunciated each word as one spoke to a child. With a huff, he turned on his heel and marched out of the parlor, slamming the door to his study somewhere deeper in the house.

Elizabeth closed her eyes and thanked Providence for the strength to defy the man responsible for ruining her perfect life in Hertfordshire. A sob behind her made Elizabeth turn around and immediately she rushed to embrace her friend.

"Ssh, ssh, he's gone now Charlotte. No harm will come."

"I was foolish to write you. My father left and would not allow Maria to stay beyond his visit. When they left, I was rash and sent for you."

"I am here now. Your letter was a happy coincidence." Elizabeth smiled at her friend with a cat caught the mouse look.

"Happy? I brought you here and you shall be miserable. He will not relent you see, now that you have challenged him." Charlotte's eyes widened in fear. But her friend shook her head.

"There are matters I cannot tell you, but I promise you when my time here is over, say the word and I will take you with me." Elizabeth searched Charlotte's face for understanding but could find none. With a heavy heart, she hugged her friend once more and changed the subject to more mundane matters.

As the two women took the stairs to Elizabeth's guest room, Charlotte explained the biggest mystery in her life involved the chickens. The stress of the arrival and confrontation with Mr. Collins bubbled over and both women were laughing until they cried as Charlotte described her visions of a masterful egg thief. For a moment as Elizabeth began to inspect Anna's unpacking of her trunks in the rose themed room, it felt like just a year ago when the two of them had not a care in the world.

"Lizzie, why did you come to Kent so quickly? You must have scarcely received my letter before you began to travel."

Elizabeth carefully moved her folio of letters and correspondence from the desk drawer back to the false bottom of her trunk. There were items in there she would not wish to see fall into the wrong hands.

"I cannot tell you all, Charlotte, but soon. I promise."

"You're not in any kind of trouble are you? Without a home?"

Elizabeth swallowed hard. So the news of her dismissal from Longbourn had reached her friend's ears, though what could she expect. The whole neighborhood likely gossiped about the unruly Bennet daughter finally reaping her oats.

"I am well. My aunt and uncle provide me a good home. But when the opportunity to travel presented itself, I can say I was most pleased for a brief change in scenery."

Charlotte Collins crossed her arms and waited. "How did you have the funds, if you do not mind me asking?"

To see Charlotte so serious, Elizabeth nearly doubled over once more in a fit of manic laughter. But this was a serious matter, indeed, and her friend was not being nosy, but careful. A single woman in possession of money to travel while estranged from her family usually meant only one occupation. Charlotte busied herself with seeing the bed was properly made for her guest.

"Promise you won't tell?" Elizabeth whispered, making Charlotte panic slightly at the potential truth of her friend's situation. "I do sums for my Uncle's business."

"Lizzie!" Charlotte picked up a pillow from her friend's bed and slammed it down in annoyance.

"What? You insinuated . . ."

"I certainly did not!"

The two girls collapsed onto the bed and like times where they had lounged in one another's parlors or bedrooms as children reading, their heads touched, but no other part. Both looking up at the ceiling, the weight of their situations pressed all around them.

"I am not so very unhappy . . ."

"Don't. You owe me no explanation. And while I can do nothing about that weasel at the moment, I shall at least find a way to help you with the chickens to catch the thief."

"The masterful egg thief," Charlotte corrected.

"Yes, we shall catch the entire gang of egg thieves."

Chapter Ten

Elizabeth Bennet strolled confidently down the manicured garden rows on the south side of the Rosings estate. The morning sun lifted her spirits and she giggled, wondering how long it would take Mr. Darcy to find her in their impromptu game of hide-go-seek. Feeling perfectly private and alone, Elizabeth untied her bonnet and skipped merrily down the pristine lawn to the end of the hedge.

A tall man stepped out from the shadow cast by the low angle of the new sun. Elizabeth rushed forward to crash into his torso. But Mr. Darcy held his arms out to stop her, making Elizabeth frown.

"Not here, not yet. The southern side of the gardens is easily spotted from the main house. But come and I shall show you my favorite glen from when I was a boy and hiding from my aunt and parents." Darcy reached out to clasp her hand and began walking her further and further away from the estate house.

"Do you mean to say, sir, you were not always so fastidious in your responsibilities?"

Mr. Darcy looked over his shoulder with an expression echoing the mischievous boy he had once been. "Miss Bennet, you have no inkling of how mischievous the Fitzwilliam boys can be."

"But you are a Darcy. I am confident I should have no fears." Her voice wavered as the surroundings became more dense forest and rustic. In the back of her mind, years of being raised to play the perfect young lady with manners above reproach screamed at the danger she was placing herself in.

Reaching a copse of trees where the grass seemed perfectly encircled Darcy walked her towards a large tree and pressed himself against her as he claimed her lips. Elizabeth dropped her bonnet and tangled her hands in the man's luscious locks, eager to claim more and more of him, yet uncertain as to how. Swooning under his kiss, she heard and felt him give a guttural growl, a primal sound that increased the tension in her lower belly.

"Mr. Darcy . . ." she said breathlessly as his kisses traveled her jawline, her neck, and to the small shallow of her collarbone.

"Elizabeth, you drive me mad." He managed to say between his attentions to her delicate ivory skin.

"Please, I need . . ." Elizabeth's mind struggled to voice what she desired. All of those weeks being separated, all of those months of pining for Mr. Darcy's touch and company. Now she had the man, in as private a location as they could manage, and she had no idea what was possible.

Fitzwilliam's hand slid from her lower back around to the front, resting for a moment against her abdomen. Gingerly, his hand slid higher and higher up her form. When his large hand finally cupped her breast, Elizabeth gasped and he immediately dropped his hand and walked away a few steps.

"Forgive me. I am a beast . . ."

"No, Fitzwilliam." She took a few steadying breaths then stepped towards him. As she touched her hand to his shoulder, he rebuffed her efforts by shaking his upper body away. The coldness made her shiver.

A Virtue of Marriage

"I cannot, that is, I was wanton and I do not blame you for wishing to abandon me."

"Abandon you?" He turned around and searched her face with his own crumpled in fear. "I needed a moment to calm myself." Darcy reached forward to clasp her hand and kissed the bare skin. Elizabeth had not bothered to don gloves when the weather was so warm. "I despise this playacting we must employ, but in speaking with Richard last night, we cannot execute our plan until next week when the Archbishop of Canterbury arrives on his tour of the country."

"The Arch . . . Archbishop?" Elizabeth knees weakened a moment at mention of the man. How did Fitzwilliam expect to convince the highest man in the Church of England to marry his cousins?

"He is my godfather. Richard spoke to his office in London and as his family has aligned with mine since ancient times, he is in favor of our scheme. Especially since Richard produced letters from Anne expressing her intentions."

"But will he truly agree to marry them? I worry he will side with Lady Catherine and all will be lost."

Darcy laughed and offered his arm to his Elizabeth. "His Grace eloped with his own wife decades ago. My father may or may not have assisted his old schoolmate from Cambridge."

Elizabeth shook her head, highly amused by the improper behavior of the higher classes. If her father were here he would be most thoroughly diverted by such tales, she thought wistfully, before a wave of melancholy washed over her heart.

"Fitzwilliam, about my behavior before, I must insist you allow my apologies."

"Elizabeth Bennet, my darling and my life, from this moment forward, please set aside the strictures of society. Any affections or liberties you allow are a balm to my injured heart."

"Truly?" She stopped their progress and turned to look at him. Sadly they were now within the view of the main house, and Darcy could not kiss his intended.

He nodded and gulped as his mouth positively salivated over the woman before him. It was his deepest desire to carry her off to his carriage and not stop until they reached Gretna Green. "One week. It is unbearable to be sure, but then we shall return to Hertfordshire and seek your father's blessing."

Elizabeth leaned slightly into his arm as they continued to walk, but when reaching the split between the main path towards Rosings and the small footbridge to the parsonage, Elizabeth released her hold on him.

A Virtue of Marriage

"Shall I not walk you to the parsonage?"

"No." Elizabeth frowned as her answer vexed even her, but she turned towards Fitzwilliam to explain. "My cousin is suspicious and I fear he shall run to tell Lady Catherine both what is true and fabricated in his mind. Perhaps we ought to limit our walks together in the future as well." Elizabeth said, tasting a bitter bile rise up in her mouth. Her heart ached when she was separated from Fitzwilliam, but they were so close to their aims, so close to freeing him from his family's clutches.

Tears pricking her eyes, she spun away from Fitzwilliam. "We mustn't do anything to jeopardize your scheme. I could not bear to lose you now, and I do not trust myself alone in your company."

The confession of her desire for him seized Darcy's lungs. The overwhelming need to capture this beguiling woman again flooded his senses, but as he pinched his eyes closed, a voice of reason stalled his impulsivity. Elizabeth glanced over her shoulder and misread his expression.

"I have spoken out of turn, offended you."

"No, no, would you please stop thinking the worst? Your honesty pains me, but not in the way you believe, madam. It pains me that I am not free in my abilities to provide for and protect you. And most of all, to love you."

The last words between the couple hung in the air as the only comfort they could give before finally walking away from the path. Elizabeth carefully retied her bonnet and used a furtive look over her shoulder to glance at the handsome form her Mr. Darcy cut as he walked away. Relishing such a blissful yet bittersweet morning amble, she momentarily forgot the nightmare of her accommodations as she entered the parsonage.

Chapter Eleven

Finding Charlotte in the kitchen with the cook, Elizabeth helped herself to an apple from the bowl on the table.

"Lizzie. You should hurry upstairs, Mr. Collins will return in a moment from his meeting with Mr. Hobbs."

Elizabeth shrugged, and continued to chew her apple, eliciting an exasperated sigh from Charlotte.

"He is always unhappy when he returns from his meeting with Mr. Hobbs. They are touring the glebe lands today. And he left without breaking his fast, so cook and I are preparing a glorious meal." Charlotte's face glowed with the achievement of her dearest dream, to run a household all her own with everything properly in order.

"If you ask me, Mr. Collins is always unhappy regardless of the situation," Elizabeth said, noticing the cook paused in her stirring and her shoulders shook in silent laughter.

"Please. He is not all bad, no one is. We are newly married and there is an adjustment period."

Elizabeth finished her apple and opened the back door to toss the waste on the composting pile in the corner of the garden.

"I will repair my appearance if it shall make you happy, but not for him."

Elizabeth left the kitchens just as a dark parson's hat walked past the front windows. Cringing, she tried to quicken her steps to reach the stairs, but only managed to the landing before the front door opened.

Placing his hat on the hook in the hall, Collins immediately called out to his cousin.

"You look afright this morning, Cousin Elizabeth, and are those grass stains on your hem and boots?"

"Yes, I was outside just now to discard an apple core, if you must know. I am returning above stairs to restore my appearance for the morning meal." Elizabeth curtseyed and again tried to leave his presence.

"Fine. Fine. I will have you understand while you are under my roof, there is to be none of that walking on a whim you are so fond of. This is not your father's land, and even there, I questioned the wisdom of such freedoms given to young ladies of weaker mind. No, I wish to make it perfectly clear that while you are present, you shall comport yourself with the utmost decency and decorum as Lady Catherine has come to expect of my humble family. Am I understood?"

"Perfectly, sir." Elizabeth pursed her lips, defying his very edict with her delightful memories of this morning's ramble with her Mr. Darcy. Oh, if Collins knew the liberties she had allowed, he would likely throw her out of the house this instant!

"Good. Now, see about your hair as well, Cousin. I will not have any of those sloppy London fashions in this household. Lady Catherine might visit at any moment should we be so lucky to receive her benevolence."

Elizabeth said nothing and walked up the stairs. Once in her room, she cradled her stomach and breathed in deeply. So many thoughts rushed through her mind as she wondered what on earth had possessed her to behave so abominably this morning? Yes, Fitzwilliam said he enjoyed her attentions, but her uncle's warning about extending her reputation to bounds of propriety rang in her ears.

Spying her haphazard appearance in the looking glass, she resolved to check her desires and behave properly no matter what circumstances befell her. Only one week and she and Fitzwilliam could run away to Hertfordshire and she would finally be one step closer to reclaiming her old life.

Chapter Twelve

Netherfield Park bustled with activity as the master and his new mistress were finally home as far as the staff was concerned. Jane Bingley steadied her breath, gazing out over the grand entryway, remembering the home alight with glorious candlelight the evening of her engagement ball. She nodded at a number of maids and footmen she had long since known growing up in the village together. Elegantly descending the stairs, she had an appointment with Mrs. Cunningham in the dining room to inspect the silver.

A few new faces made her uneasy, but for the most part she felt confident in her role as Mistress of Netherfield Park. The only hitch in her peaceful existence was educating Miss Caroline Bingley as to the changes in the household she wished to affect. One week home in Hertfordshire and she sorely regretted offering Charles' unmarried sister a visit to the estate. It made no sense that the young woman was heart-set on returning to the country just at the height of the Season in London. But Jane was unprepared to parry her sister-in-law's manipulations when they rested for a day at the Hurst town home on their trek home from Bath.

After inspecting the silver service, Jane set the perfectly polished spoon down upon the table and nodded to Mrs. Cunningham. "Please tell the maids I am most pleased with their efforts. Their work has not gone unnoticed in supporting my first dinner party as Mr. Bingley's wife."

"Yes ma'am. The girls will be happy to hear they pleased you."

"Has the meat arrived from Mr. Alberts?"

"Aye ma'am, Cook has the supplies downstairs as we speak."

Jane stared out the dining room window at the expansive grounds beyond bursting with spring bounty. It was the first morning since their return that her husband had dressed and sought a morning ride. He promised Jane to seek a mount for her use so that she might join him in enjoying her home countryside. One of the few Bennet girls who dearly loved to ride, her family's horses had often been needed in the fields. Jane turned her attentions back to the housekeeper.

"Shall we go to the kitchens then?" Jane held up her hand as the housekeeper began to politely protest. "Fear not, Mrs. Cunningham, this is not to find fault. I merely wish to see that all is well and there is no detail I cannot see to." Jane Bingley offered her housekeeper a shy smile, a rare occurrence in all of Mrs. Cunningham's years. She had heard the Bennet girls were raised in a household where the servants were considered family, but in all her years of serving London's elite, she had never seen such manners.

"As you wish, Madam." Mrs. Cunningham motioned for the footman to open the door to admit Mrs. Bingley down towards the servant areas in the kitchens below.

To most it would appear as only perfect cracks in the wall, but then again, Jane was learning Netherfield Park had numerous improvements her family home of Longbourn could neither afford nor institute with it's Tudor-styled layout. Not a day went by that Charles did not speak of the dreams he held in building their own home. But Jane was not so sure all of their leased estate's features would make her list of necessary amenities. She did not like secret doors and hidden halls.

With Mrs. Bingley on her way to the kitchen, Mrs. Cunningham instructed the footman to carefully restore the silver to its proper storage when Miss Bingley strolled into the dining room. Shoulders back, nose in the air, Caroline did not so much as deign to acknowledge the servants of the room before hastily snatching a fork off the table and holding it up to the light of the window. With an exaggerated huff, she finally looked to the housekeeper.

"Do not tell me this service is what you intend to show Mrs. Bingley as passing muster for her first dinner party! Why this fork is positively filthy." Caroline released the fork from her hand so it tumbled to the table.

In months past, Mrs. Cunningham feared angering the sister of Mr. Bingley. The entire staff walked on eggshells to avoid being fired on the spot, many times without notice. Netherfield's staffing situation had become so alarming that it impaired Mrs. Cunningham's ability to attract proper candidates when posts were emptied.

"Mrs. Bingley herself just approved the service, Miss Bingley. Perhaps if you would like to make your opinions known to her, I should be happy to instruct the maids to polish once more if my mistress requests." Mrs. Cunningham smiled sweetly at Caroline.

"You're telling me a falsehood. No mistress of the house would approve such shoddy work. I'm off to find my sister-in-law at this moment to disprove your lies."

The housekeeper nodded towards the footman who again opened the secret door to the kitchens. Caroline cocked her head to one side and folded her arms in front of her chest, clearly confused at the movement.

"Mrs. Bingley went to see to the kitchens not a moment ago. I'm certain you might catch her if you'd like." Mrs. Cunningham extended her arm with an open hand to invite Miss Bingley down to the kitchens, a place she knew the young woman only went when absolutely forced to go.

"That's quite all right, I shall wait for her in the sitting room. Or perhaps I shall go inspect the suites above stairs. With this weather, one can never be sure if guests will be remaining with our family overnight." Caroline said through clenched teeth and stormed out of the dining room. She did not add she would bet that Mrs. Bennet would find some trifling reason to extend their stay, and that she'd risk money on that eventuality if she only had anyone with which to make such a wager. As Caroline Bingley stormed the stairs, she felt the closest emotion to missing her own sister, Louisa, as she could.

The former mistress of Netherfield Park had left the dining room for not a moment before the poor young footman began to snicker. Mrs. Cunningham gave him a sharp look, then found herself highly amused as well. The new Mrs. Bingley might be sweet and serene as could be, but in a test of wills, Cunningham's loyalties lay firmly in belief the Bennet girl could soundly trounce the Bingley one.

Chapter Thirteen

The knocker at Number Twelve Grosvenor Square stood restored post haste of the Wickhams' first outing to the theater. Georgiana Wickham admitted the most exalted ladies of the Ton, thinking herself the most proper social hostess in London. It was only on the third of such days that she suspected she was quickly becoming London's biggest laugh behind ornate fans in every ballroom.

"Mrs. Wickham, I do beg your pardon." Miss Sarah Milbanke, the niece of the formidable Lady Cowper, intently gazed at the young woman in front of her.

Georgiana looked up from staring at the tiny teaspoon stirring her tea. The silver Darcy crest on the end had captured her imagination. She had wondered at the level of the craftsman who fashioned such a true likeness to the three cinquefoils clearly distinguished in the field of crosses.

"Forgive me, you were speaking of my husband?"

"Yes. I was remarking on how quiet you managed to keep your engagement, and yet here you tell me you are married almost a year come this summer!"

Georgiana focused with all of her might to not squirm as a pupil under the interrogation of a tutor. She was the married woman in the room, though Miss Milbanke's recent engagement to Lord Strange, the eldest son of the Earl of Derby, gave her an air of superiority over Georgiana. She had to hold the line of her matrimonial rank, even if she would never hold a courtesy title from the peerage from her marriage.

"We kept it strictly a family affair and my George and I were married at the seaside. My brother Fitzwilliam stood up for George."

It was a lie, but it was the falsehood Colonel Fitzwilliam and her brother had taught her for the day when questions of her marriage would arise. Confess to first a secret marriage, and that they had the second ceremony later for family in London.

"How is dear Fitzwilliam? I have not seen him since the Cowpers' ball to end last Season. I heard rumors he killed some poor girl in the back country with his horse."

Georgiana took a meditated sip from her now perfectly cool tea. She frowned about his trip to Hertfordshire, an event she still felt a strong signal that her brother did not truly care in the least for her. She had eloped and he had not come after her, not like her other guardian, Colonel Fitzwilliam. Georgiana decided a change in subject was warranted.

George had said Anne's demise was nearing, and her last letter from her brother did relate even he thought the situation was dire. Surely there could be nothing wrong with finally telling the truth of her brother's coming marriage and impending widower status?

"He is in Kent attending to our ailing cousin, Anne."

Miss Milbanke feigned a small smile at the heroics of Darcy. She had never deigned to chase the elusive Dark Man of Derbyshire, but she had plenty of unattached friends who would crow for this information. "Dear me, I hope it is not too serious."

"On the contrary, Anne is dying." Georgiana added another biscuit to her plate, then scolded herself because it would be her third one this morning.

"I say, shouldn't you also be there to tend to your cousin at this trying time?"

Georgiana shook her head, as her mouth was full from failing to resist the pastry. Miss Milbanke waited patiently as Georgiana washed down the remaining crumbs in her mouth with another gulp of tea.

"Brother wished for me and George to stay here. Our presence would not please my aunt, Lady Catherine, you see." Georgiana cringed anticipating a question from the opening she just gave.

"Oh you poor dear, ordered away from your cousin that forgive me, we all knew suffered so painfully during her short life. It speaks very highly that your brother shows such family devotion."

Georgiana inhaled a breath of relief that Sarah hadn't asked her to clarify how she and her husband wouldn't please her aunt. Without thinking, Georgiana eagerly corrected her impression of why Fitzwilliam was in Kent.

"But Fitzwilliam must be there! Anne is to be his wife, they are to marry any day now." Finishing her biscuit, Georgiana missed the slightest signs of shock as Sarah Milbanke's cheeks reddened and her nostrils flared.

After a few seconds of silence, Georgiana glanced at the clock to see if the hour was near to end tea. She had tired of Miss Milbanke's company even though George was most earnest to receive an invite to a dinner party next week to be hosted by Lord Strange.

"George Wickham," Sarah Milbanke mused. "Isn't he the heir to the Duke of Devonshire?"

On impulse, Georgiana giggled. How could this woman not know that it was the Cavendish family who fulfilled the dukedom? Even she, nearly sixteen, wasn't so base as to not study the peerage lines.

"While His Grace is an acquaintance of my family, my husband is much closer in familiarity. His father was my father's steward." Georgiana beamed with pride that her husband had been mistaken for the heir to a dukedom. She would be sure to tell him about the funny mistaken identity.

"Pardon me, once more, but did I hear correctly? You married your steward's son?"

Georgiana's bubble of pride popped. "Er, no, Old Mr. Wickham was a steward to my father, but not our current steward. George was educated at Cambridge with my brother. He is a gentleman in all that matters!"

Sarah Milbanke snorted as she placed her cup of tea on the small consort table before her. As she donned her gloves, Georgiana noticed the clear cue that the social call was over and she knew George would be upset with her that she hadn't obtained an invitation to the Stanley family dinner party. Summoning up her courage, Georgiana made one last desperate move to please her husband.

"Miss Milbanke, I thought to host a dinner party and hoped to send you and Lord Strange an invitation."

As Miss Milbanke rose, she tightened her lips into a most displeasing line, though her eyes showed a small amount of sympathy to the young woman before her treading water far deeper than her head. "I'm sorry, I believe we have a previous engagement that evening. You understand, with the wedding a mere two months away, my calendar is full to the brim since the Earl of Derby and his family's connections are so vast."

"Certainly, such a lengthy engagement must be a taxing social endeavor. I was never formally out before finding my true love, and thankfully spared your burden." Georgiana showed sympathy back to the older woman before her, hoping her comment didn't offend.

"I shall bear my burden with the bravest face . . ." Sarah Milbanke paused to walk towards the foyer and turned around as they reached the door "and the loveliest gowns!" Both women laughed at her tease, though Georgiana's laughter was forced politeness.

It wasn't until after Sarah Milbanke was handed into her carriage with the most scandalous intelligence of the Darcy family and Georgiana climbed the stairs to rest in her suite that she realized her invitation was spurned without a set date. Concrete she was too stupid to even notice a cut as it hit her during tea time, Mrs. Wickham collapsed onto her bed and cried.

Chapter Fourteen

Dawn greeted Elizabeth Bennet with a mission. Rising with the sun, she set out to learn the truth behind the mystery of the chickens only producing a fraction of the eggs one would expect from the brood the parsonage kept. Wrapping herself in a shawl and wearing her weathered boots, she tiptoed from her guest room. Now three days since her arrival, it was the first morning she felt confident of the household routine to escape unnoticed.

The young maid Eileen cleaned and assisted in the parsonage, but as her elder sister worked at Rosings, Elizabeth felt that she could not trust the young lass to agree to her plan to stalk the chicken coop. Rather than test the girl,

Elizabeth saved her from ever making a choice by keeping the maid as much out of her affairs as was humanly possible. And Anna, being a guest servant, but not quite truly Elizabeth's own maid, did not need to get into any mischief. No, the chicken investigation would by necessity be a one-woman operation.

With the early glow on the horizon, Elizabeth waited in the dusky shades of the retreating night in a darkened corner of the hencoop. She had to stoop low, but her small frame allowed her to enter the vile smelling cranny with minimal fuss from the chickens as she was not above collecting their labors herself shortly after the sun rose. Animals know a person accustomed to their keep and care.

Her stealth paid off in but minutes when a young boy of about eight poked his head right in and lifted an egg from a vacated nest right in front of her eyes.

"Ooooo! So you're the thief!" Elizabeth chuckled but scared the poor boy right out of his wits. After making a startled yelp, the boy began running away. "Wait!"

All of the commotion caused an uproar in the previously docile chickens, making them flap and squawk and attack Elizabeth as she tried to maneuver out of the small coop. Feathers and muck flew in the air. Gashing her hand against the rough wooden frame on her way out, she paused a second to see which way the boy ran, and seeing some tall weeds moving rapidly to her east, she also took off running.

Years of walking and occasionally, unladylike running, made Elizabeth far faster than the poor boy and she caught up to him just as he was crossing a glebe field and dashed into the small copse of woods that lined the southern edge of Rosings. Elizabeth had never ventured in this direction before, as she had yet to meet the tenants of the glebe lands. Barred from her "rambles" as both a practical rule and one of the great indignities Mr. Collins imposed to exert control over his cousin, the unfamiliarity of the lands began to worry her conscience more than the senseless rule.

"Please, wait, I shall not hurt you. But I am unfamiliar with these parts and I will become lost without your aid." She called after the boy who paused and looked surprisingly at Elizabeth so close behind him.

"You run fast, miss!"

Elizabeth smiled. "We haven't been properly introduced." Elizabeth wiped her hand on her apron and noticed the nasty gash between her thumb and her forefinger. A healthy amount of blood mixed in with the dirt and likely chicken droppings smeared on her hand, making even

Elizabeth repulsed at the idea of touching it. She shook her hand loosely and nodded to the boy. "I am Elizabeth Bennet. My cousin is Pastor Collins, the manager of these lands."

"Peter Holbein, ma'am." He gave a small bow and grinned, showing missing teeth in the top of his mouth next to his front two teeth.

"Mr. Holbein, may I count on you for assistance? I injured my hand back there and need desperately to clean the wound."

"Our cottage is just around here." He pointed further into the copse of trees, and Elizabeth tried to follow the direction of his hand, but it was pointless. All she could see was the forest becoming denser and a narrow footpath before her.

"Well, I should have to trust your lead, sir."

Peter grinned at Elizabeth and marched on at a quick pace, though not trying to lose her, but just urge her to hurry with him towards help. Before long, they stood in front of a modest home with the prettiest brook off to the northern edge of it. Elizabeth recognized at once where she was as she saw the drive lead through another copse of woods back toward the main road to the proper village of Hunsford. She remembered the bridge crossing on her arrival, but had no idea this picturesque cottage lie just minutes away and on lands controlled by her cousin.

"Hurry inside, miss. Mama is a right good healer. She takes care of all my scrapes." Peter gave another broad grin, still holding possessively to the one egg he managed to nick that morning.

Elizabeth took notice of his stolen treasure, reminding herself she wasn't completely happy with this boy and had to speak with his parents about his thievery of Charlotte's eggs, but first she needed to clean her hand as quickly as possible before it made her ill.

"Perhaps you should go inside first and let your Mama know I have called." Elizabeth shifted her weight from foot to foot, feeling far more the horrific stranger for calling at such an ungodly early hour and not as a gentlewoman related to the manager of the lands the Holbeins leased.

Peter nodded and ducked his head inside the plain wooden door. He had hardly closed it when he heard him yell for his mother. In a few moments, the door swung open quickly; revealing a woman not too much older than Elizabeth with long, thin auburn hair and a belly full with child. Her dress was clearly on a turn and looked to be nearly ready for the rag pile.

Elizabeth quickly dropped to a curtsy for the woman who did her best to respond, though given her condition managed not much more than a slight knee bend.

"Oh please, I am so sorry for the inconvenience. You see I ran into young Peter at my cousin's chicken coop this morning and I injured my hand..."

"Come in, come in Miss Bennet." The woman smiled much like her son, and Elizabeth couldn't help but be calmed by the resemblance, though Peter's hair was a dark brown. "Petey told me all about it and I must say, I've been so very thankful for the work your cousin be letting him do."

Confused, Elizabeth followed Mrs. Holbein into the snug home that consisted of a main open room with a single door on the back end. Stairs led to a lofted area above, where she supposed Peter slept. A young girl, perhaps two or three, sat on a ratty rug in front of the fireplace and sucked on her two first fingers on her right hand in comfort. Mrs. Holbein stooped down and scooped the young girl up, turning to present her to Elizabeth.

"This here is my youngest, Mary Jane."

Elizabeth was delighted to hear the young girl's name and shared she had two sisters of those very same names. The young girl pulled out her fingers and gave a toothy smile and then shocked Elizabeth by responding.

"My name is for my aunties who are in heaven." The young girl promptly returned her fingers to her mouth and Elizabeth raised an eyebrow. Perhaps she was not so young as she was just simply small.

Mrs. Holbein poured some of the water set to boil for breakfast into a basin and added cool water from the pump. A small sliver of lye soap on the sink joined the bowl at the plain wooden table and Mrs. Holbein directed Elizabeth to it.

"Mrs. Holbein–"

"Please, call me Diana."

Elizabeth smiled and then grimaced as the woman plunged her hand into the basin and began vigorously scrubbing at the dirt and grime caked onto the skin. She sucked in her breath and then felt an odd sensation on her leg. She looked down and saw the petite hand of Mary Jane touching her knee to calm her as the girl looked up dolefully from the floor, her fingers of comfort still in place. Before Elizabeth could say anything, the sharp pain stopped as Diana had wrapped her hand in a fresh towel and beckoned Peter to dispose of the water outside.

Protectively holding her hand, as it still stung from the fresh cleaning, Elizabeth addressed the woman and thanked her for her help.

"Twas nothing, Miss Bennet. The least I could do for all of your family's generosity."

A Virtue of Marriage

"Now, you must call me Elizabeth if I'm to call you Diana." Elizabeth paused; slightly perturbed at the number of liberties she was breaking by first imposing on this woman at such an early hour and now calling her by her Christian name, but was rapidly making up for it in reciprocating the offer. While she had fully planned to take Peter to task for his misdeeds, the family living inside of the cottage made her pause before jumping to a decision. But she felt most unpleasant there was a falsehood afoot about the source of eggs Peter was bringing home, and she would remedy reality to the truth, one way or the other. "Is your husband already at work in the fields?"

"Nay, he's still resting but should awake in an hour or so when the drink wears off."

Again shocked by the honesty of Mrs. Holbein, Elizabeth squirmed at the mention of Mr. Holbein's drunkenness. "I am so sorry to hear of his affliction." She looked down at the table, trying to formulate a solution to her current predicament.

"Oh no miss, he's no devil of a man. The ale lets him sleep what little comfort he can. Last fall, a tree fell on him, as he's a lumberjack. It nearly killed him. Broke his back, I say. He's been stuck up in a bed for months and the pain just makes him moan and moan. I worked as a launderer until I became too far along with this one, the babe the Good Lord blessed us with before my husband turned ill. Our last I suppose, as my good John cannot walk on his own." Diana rubbed her protruding belly as she told her tale and Elizabeth felt heartsick.

"Forgive me, but what has your family subsided on?" Elizabeth naturally reached down to little Mary Jane, still playing at her feet and planted the young girl onto her lap. Mary Jane twisted around and looked up at her new friend with the trust only a child can bestow. With a happy sigh, the little girl rested her head against Elizabeth's shoulder.

"We had some money saved up, and there was the firewood John had cut for us that I was able to sell. I wrote to his cousin Peter as well, as some of John's family came to England before we did, and I suspect he will send some aid soon."

Mrs. Holbein began to pour in oats to make a large bowl of porridge when Peter came running in, releasing his stolen treasure to his mother.

"Sorry Mama, I only collected one this morning before bringing Elizabeth to get help for her hand."

Diana patted his head and took the egg as a most precious cargo. She cracked it gently and dropped it in the boiling water before wiping her hands on her apron. Her work made Elizabeth remember she would be missed before too long and had to leave.

Spying young Peter shift nervously at the corner of the kitchen area, Elizabeth sat up taller as she realized how she could help. She caught his eye and winked, making the boy with a gaunt face, now that she took proper stock of him, open his mouth in a surprised 'o' shape before pressing it closed again.

"If you can spare Peter for a little more time this morning, I have a few more tasks he can help me with Mrs. Holbein." In her fib, Elizabeth forgot to use Diana's Christian name, but hoped the flaw wouldn't be noticed.

"Absolutely, Miss Bennet." No such luck and Elizabeth realized her mistake re-established her superior social class to the Holbeins though that was not her intention.

Diana turned to Peter to address him after opening the larder to hand him the moldiest piece of bread Elizabeth had ever seen. Forgetting she might offend the woman further, Elizabeth stepped in to promise to break Peter's fast at her own kitchens as soon as they arrived.

With nothing more to do than to take her leave, Elizabeth marched back across the fields soaked in dew with young Master Holbein at her side. Her anger at the poor family's situation rose as a bitter taste in the back of her throat, but she refused to let it rule her reasoning.

"Mr. Holbein, while I appreciate the measures you felt necessary to save your family by stealing my cousin's eggs, nevertheless a thief holds no honor. You may have eggs and other food as they can provide, but you will report here each morning to help with the chores in payment for the assistance."

Peter's eyes lit up. "You are offering me work, Elizabeth?"

"Well no, not a permanent position, but there will just be no more stealing food that rightfully belongs to Mr. Collins. You may earn food to eat, but never take." Elizabeth noticed the young boy walking a touch taller in response to her admonishment and assignation of enough age to earn his keep. Her own stomach gave a lurch from the hours of consciousness with no nourishment, and she wondered if the Holbein children only received one meal a day, as it would not be inconsistent with the state of the larder she saw.

Approaching the parsonage, Elizabeth could see heavy smoke rising from the chimney, telling her the kitchen staff of two was awake and well. She motioned for Peter to follow her through the small herb garden to the side door and wait for her on the stoop.

Cook promptly assisted Elizabeth as soon as she stepped in the door with the removal of her shawl, deference Elizabeth always appreciated from her one ally in the home.

"Missus, you would not believe! Eileen found six eggs this morn, the chickens are healed!"

Elizabeth rolled her eyes and washed her hands in the basin near the sink just for this purpose. "It was less the chickens than a hungry family."

Cook's eyes widened at the threat of treacherous theft, but Elizabeth approached the older woman and patted her arm.

"All is well. But please, gather any food and supplies we can spare until Charlotte and I go to market tomorrow. Give them to the young boy outside the door as quickly as you can." Elizabeth smoothed her work dress and debated if she should retire upstairs to try and clean up further or just wait until later when she was to visit Anne de Bourgh with Charlotte. "We have a Christian duty to uphold."

On this last proclamation, Mr. Collins appeared in the doorway to the kitchen, inquisitive to his cousin's health. As she replied in the positive, he next asked her about the Christian duty she was most involved in this morning by her conversation with Cook.

Elizabeth expertly gave a slight nod to reinforce her pleas and escorted her cousin to the dining room where they joined his wife Charlotte to take their breakfast together. As she poured herself a cup of tea, she decided fortune favored the bold and asked Mr. Collins about the Holbein family. Perhaps he was unaware of how dire their predicament truly stood.

"Ah, the recusants. Have no fear Cousin Elizabeth, Lady Catherine and I are hard at work on removing their non-conforming family from the haven of our lands so that a more deserving family might benefit from the magnificent bounty of the Rosings."

Elizabeth nearly dropped her cup, but recovered well enough to make it to the table and sit down. Her head was spinning. The poor family she met only this morning was to endure more hardship, and at the hands of her bombastic cousin? Her kin? No, no it could not come to pass!

"But the father of the family is gravely ill, he broke his back last year in your service! Surely allowances must be made for their lack of attendance at church services." Elizabeth had no doubt with the last name, they were likely Catholic. But still, she had to hope that with proper guidance and encouragement, they could convert. After all, they left their homeland to live

A Virtue of Marriage

so far away; surely their plan was to conform before John Holbein's accident.

"They failed to make their rent payments last quarter and Mr. Hobbs informed me earlier this week they have not paid this quarter's and have no intention to settle their debts. An eviction notice is underway." Mr. Collins calmly opened his napkin as the breakfast dishes arrived to the table from the kitchen and he dug into his simple omelet with abandon.

Usually disgusted by her cousin's lack of table manners, Elizabeth sat more appalled at the fate to befall the Holbein family. She picked at her breakfast, despite being very hungry earlier.

"Remember we are to read to Miss de Bourgh this afternoon, Lizzie? She finds such comfort in the sermons." Charlotte tried to change the subject but she was too late. Mr. Collins interjected his own investigation.

"How did you come to know of the Holbein family? And why is there a bandage on your hand?" Mr. Collins did not wait to swallow his food before interrogating his cousin as to her whereabouts that morning.

"I was collecting eggs from the coop when I met their son, Peter, looking for work in exchange for food." Elizabeth lied, but also revealed a truth to her cousin. "I told him I would gladly see he could perform chores for food and

I accompanied him home to learn the situation of the family for myself, to ensure there was not more help we needed to offer."

"You walked across two fields and the woods to their cottage?"

Elizabeth nodded, knowing she was forbidden to take such a ramble without informing her cousin, but decided it to be better for her to take on the transgression than to reveal young Peter's lack of morality.

"Well I am astonished, my cousin, that again, you would directly disobey me." Mr. Collins wiped his mouth with his hand before pounding his fist on the table. "I am already confirmed that my gross negligence of your manners and behaviors has led to Lady Catherine's extreme displeasure in your reputation."

Elizabeth perhaps should have winced if she had felt a true shame for her love of Fitzwilliam Darcy, but as she did not, she didn't feel any guilt towards a scandalous affair that had yet to occur. Her lack of repentance while a great mark towards her lack of practice in deception was a less than encouraging sign to Mr. Collins.

"It appears you need further reminder that in this household, you are expected to behave with the highest modicum of propriety. That as a parson's relation, and under my protection, you may not traipse about the countryside as some country miss without a responsibility in the world—"

"But Cousin Collins, I felt a responsibility to the family on your glebe lands. I did not know you were in the process of evicting them from their cottage, though it pains my sensibilities to see children so hungry."

Elizabeth had miscalculated. She did not know the upbraiding Mr. Collins experienced from Lady Catherine over her mere arrival at Rosings and the apparent warning of her clear moral failings her disappointment represented. To interrupt her cousin, while never an acceptable behavior, but one he had overlooked in the past when she played missish to his words and not his intent, pushed him over the edge.

"Mr. Collins—" Charlotte tried to speak, but he held his hand up and his wife, knowing better, obeyed.

Mr. Collins stood up and leaned over the table with both hands on either side of this plate, his knuckles white. "Elizabeth Bennet, you are on the precipice of damnation with your sins against this household, our esteemed patroness Lady Catherine, and God himself. I am remiss in my duty as your nearest male relation and pastor of this flock if I did not take a strong hand with you to correct your ways."

Elizabeth sat in shock at the man before her. Mr. Collins always held a healthy dose of the ridiculous in him, but never had she ever anticipated him to actually act the brute! The nature of this conversation was alarming indeed, and she lacked the skills to thwart it, as her father had never so much as scolded her aside from laughing at her expense.

Staring down at her plate appeared to have some effect on Mr. Collin's tirade of Scripture and other sermon notes about a dutiful woman's place in the world. In all honesty, her panics prevented her from listening further and instead assess her current limited options. If she raised the alarm now, all would be for naught. The Archbishop would not arrive for another four days' time.

"As ultimate responsibility falls to me for your very salvation, I believe you shall spend the day in your room without meals until tomorrow to finally accept your new place in the world as a poor relation reliant upon the generosity of your betters. And to consider the ramifications of your actions when you act without your family's approval and therefore the approval of the Divine."

Elizabeth's involuntary smirk was ill-timed, as even she could not believe this man truly believed she considered him, a distant cousin

A Virtue of Marriage

she had never met until last year, to represent her father's authority.

"You may begin now." Mr. Collins pushed himself away from the table and stood to brook no argument from Elizabeth, but that did not stop her from trying.

"I am to read to Miss de Bourgh today, surely you do not wish me to dissatisfy Lady Catherine . . ."

"I have no doubt the magnanimous Lady Catherine will applaud this intervention as she has pressed upon me the need to curtail your headstrong ways before they make me the laughingstock of the neighborhood."

Elizabeth had no choice but to serve out this ridiculous penance for a transgression she would never repent, but considered the days of goodwill she should reap from her cousin in granting him this one day of false obedience. After all, it's not obedience if one is compelled to comply.

"Please send my regret to Miss de Bourgh and her cousins if you visit Rosings today." Elizabeth looked to Charlotte, whose face was paler than freshly laundered linens. As Charlotte's lips trembled, Elizabeth blew out a quick breath in a whistling motion to signal all was well. Disappointment finally displayed on Elizabeth's face as she truly desired to visit with her Mr. Darcy whom she had not seen in two days.

"I most certainly shall, and remember dear cousin, excel in this to show me you acknowledge your place and you may perhaps visit the illustrious Rosings tomorrow."

As Elizabeth took each step slowly, still in shock she was in truth being sent to her room for disobedience like a child, each lifted foot reinforced that she would never have survived a marriage to this man. Furthermore, if she couldn't have survived, she had to find a way out of this disastrous union for Charlotte. Near the top of the stairs, Elizabeth comforted herself that her prison was to be her room where she had a novel, letters, and most importantly a lock on the door.

As she entered the room and swiftly turned the key to keep her meddling cousin from any second thoughts or lectures of her behavior, a deep rumble echoed in Elizabeth's belly. She was hungry, and for today, she would suffer those pangs in careful fasting for the plight of the Holbein family, who she vowed to see to happier times before rescuing her knight, Mr. Darcy.

Chapter Fifteen

Charlotte Collins' somber expression immediately deflated the jubilant mood of her friend Miss Anne de Bourgh. Charlotte bit her lower lip as Anne craned her neck to look for the arrival of Charlotte's particular friend.

"Miss Elizabeth?" Anne asked.

Charlotte slowly shook her head. "She pushed Mr. Collins too far, I'm afraid, and he ordered her locked in her room."

Anne's mouth dropped in horror at such treatment for a guest, even if she was a relation to Mr. Collins. But more than that, Anne knew they must hide Elizabeth's fate from her cousin, Mr. Darcy. Unfortunately, Anne had no time to explain the matter to Charlotte before a maid carrying refreshments entered her bedroom, followed by her cousin, himself.

Darcy bowed elegantly to the ladies and did his best to hide his own furtive glances around the room; realizing one of the ladies he expected to be in this room was not present.

"Mrs. Collins, I hope you do not mind I have taken the liberty to order some refreshments for your visit. I am afraid my aunt has been too distracted at times to offer proper courtesy to the guests of this home."

"Thank you, Mr. Darcy. I am certain your selections for comfort are very fine, indeed," Charlotte answered.

Anne took a deep breath and concentrated in speaking with a steady tone. "Mrs. Collins was just explaining to me of how her friend, Miss Bennet, came down with a rather nasty headache this morning and has decided to spend the day resting in her rooms."

Darcy looked quickly between the two ladies, concern creased in the wrinkles of his forehead. Charlotte looked to Anne for some sign of what to do about this blatant falsehood, and why on earth was she lying to Mr. Darcy about Elizabeth? Thankfully, Charlotte Collins was a smart woman and more pieces of her friend's mystery mission began to fall into place.

However, now was not the time to inquire further, so instead, Charlotte continued the charade.

"Yes, I'm afraid my friend did come down with a slight ache to her head, but I cannot be for certain it was not at least minorly exacerbated by perhaps some of the mannerisms of her own kin." Charlotte smiled and hoped Mr. Darcy would not think worse of her for speaking ill of her own husband. Instead, the man seemed to understand.

"Did your friend mention anything about wishing to visit Rosings later in her visit? I only ask because I know my cousin is most anxious to meet the woman I nearly killed with my horse. Thanks to my cousin Richard, it's become a bit of a famous story." The usually reserved Mr. Darcy nodded with a smile in his eyes for Anne who rapidly clapped her hands in appreciation.

"Yes, and Richard Fitzwilliam and I played the most delightful card game I am told she taught my sour cousin while he paid penance for his stupidity. Racing the horse on a public road, it's what you've always been warned about."

Charlotte nodded noncommittally and that seemed to be enough to soothe Mr. Darcy's inquiry. Still, with such easy manners between the men and women presumed to wed as soon as may be, Charlotte felt uneasy that such a serious question somehow involved her friend.

As a silence descended the room, Darcy realized he had been blocking the door for the poor maid stuck standing there, looking down at the carpets, during this entire conversation that did not include her. The poor little mouse did not dare to ask the great man to move out of her way, and Darcy's cheeks slightly reddened. "I believe I have overstayed my welcome, ladies, please. Please enjoy your novel, and know that hopefully more than a chapter or two might be read today."

"Fitzwilliam, how so?" Anne asked, before suffering a small coughing fit.

"Richard has invited the parson to the library for drinks. He doesn't believe me how utterly ridiculous the man can truly be." Darcy gave his cousin a sly wink and bowed once more to exit the room.

No sooner had Anne watched the door close than Mrs. Collins began to fret and wring her hands in front of her.

"Whatever is the matter, Charlotte? Don't worry, they will keep him occupied as they say."

Charlotte shook her head. "You don't understand. My husband will boast about bringing his Cousin Elizabeth in line to her ladyship's expectations. He will boast that he is starving her all day today and I'm afraid of what Mr. Darcy might do."

Anne de Bourgh's stomach felt hollow as she considered the significance of Charlotte's fears. While Charlotte only suspected a tendre existed between Mr. Darcy and her friend, Anne knew for certain. Placing her fingertips to her forehead, she pretended to swoon.

"Anne!"

Peeking her eye open, she winked at Charlotte. "Go! Tell them I fainted, I can't possibly be read to today."

"But—" Charlotte looked confused.

"Darcy loves Elizabeth. If your husband tells him he locked her up, there will be violence. Go!"

Charlotte didn't need any further encouragement. She darted out of the room and rushed down the stairs, feeling her lungs struggle with the sudden exertion. Breathless, she came upon the gentlemen in the library looking a pure fright.

"Mr. Darcy! Anne has fainted." As Charlotte leaned on the doorframe for support, she observed it wasn't Mr. Darcy that first jumped up. It was the Colonel. And the man who did not move from his comfortable chair was her own husband, who instead looked more like a deer hearing a gunshot. Charlotte caught her breath and moved out of the way so that Mr. Darcy could also leave the room, and for a brief moment, she wondered the joy she might have in widowhood if Mr. Darcy had killed her husband.

Chapter Sixteen

All of Meryton society seemed to enjoy the first dinner party thrown by the Bingley's so much so; it felt as if the wedding festivities merely continued five months after the couple's nuptials in the small village. Despite her mother's strongest attempts, her well-practiced eldest daughter appealed to her father for assistance in sending the Bennet family home at nearly two in the morning.

Exhausted, the two Bingley women agreed to Charles' invitation to the parlor for a quick nightcap.

"Charles, you cannot be serious to consider another year here. Please tell me you will give up the lease." Caroline accepted a glass of sherry

A Virtue of Marriage

from her brother and wrinkled her nose at her brief sniff of the odor.

"Caroline, this is Jane's home. We've spoken about your attitude. Why did you come to Hertfordshire? I thought you wished nothing more than to remain in London."

"Oh, well..." Caroline avoided her brother's question by trailing off with her eyes resting on the tired Jane Bingley. Sensing weakness, Caroline attacked. "What say you, dear Jane? Do you wish to keep Netherfield as your home?"

Startled, Jane struggled to remain tactful. "That is, I do love our home. But . . . I . . ."

Concerned, Bingley reached down for his wife's hand. "Dear, what is it? Tell me and I shall make you happy." He kissed her hand gallantly as Caroline rolled her eyes.

Jane sighed. "My father and mother are so angry at Lizzie, and I worry for her. She will be alone in London as soon as she returns from Kent. And I have not had one letter from her since I sent my news."

Caroline Bingley carefully inspected the finishing on the chair she sat in, intently tracing the floral pattern with her finger.

"You've had not one letter?" Charles cocked his head to one side. Elizabeth's letters arrived like clockwork when they were in Bath. It was strange indeed for no post to arrive in almost a month since they had left Bath and begun to travel; though with all of the shuffling it was possible the letters were lost.

"Not one in weeks. And . . ." Jane looked down at the carpet, ashamed to admit her distaste for her own mother. "Once my mother knows, she will become most unbearable. I should very much like to be in London when Lizzie returns from Kent."

Charles Bingley frowned. He would tell the ladies of the abuse he endured from Mr. Bennet that evening when the sexes separated after dinner. But the man's rant and accusations against his closest friend, Fitzwilliam Darcy, did not sit well with the affable Bingley. Like his Jane, he desired peace. He saw no reason why the family ostracized one daughter, for no worse sin than refusing a suitor, and fawned over another.

Setting his empty glass on the table like a judge's gavel sounding a decision had been made, the young man of not yet eight and twenty puffed his chest. "Right, so to London we go. Shall we leave on the morrow or the next day?"

Jane laughed and covered her mouth, smiling beguilingly at her husband above her. "You did always say as soon as your mind was made up you'd just as soon leave as stay."

A Virtue of Marriage

"Indeed." He bowed.

"But let's not throw the entire house into an uproar. Besides, I don't fancy sharing rooms at an inn and the Hurst town home might be a bit, imposing."

Charles blanched. He had never before had to consider travel at a moment's notice with a wife, and it jarred him that the two did not mix well. Of course he could not expect Jane to move from a large estate house to a suite of rooms! How silly she must think him!

"I shall send a letter to my solicitor to inquire about a home to lease. You are correct that I too have no desire to stay with the Hursts."

"And you Miss Bingley? Do you plan to remain with us or go back to your sister? I understand how sisterly affection might pull your heartstrings in that direction and would not feel offended if you leave us in London." Jane smiled sweetly to her sister-in-law.

Caroline left her glass for a servant to manage instead of returning it to the sideboard, and rose with a yawn. "Oh, pardon me, I am so utterly fatigued. I should hate to make you feel unsupported, Jane, in your new marriage. I suspect I shall remain with you and Charles."

The two ladies exchanged smiles; each knowing the other did not mean it. Bowing her head slightly as she announced she would retire for the evening, Caroline caught the movement of her brother's hand to Jane's midsection. Another brat was surely on its way and Caroline needed to move fast if she was to make her move on Darcy.

After locking her bedroom door and dismissing her maid, Caroline pulled a treasured teakwood box her father presented her on her sixteenth birthday from one of his business contacts. Inside held an odd assortment of items that Caroline cherished – a letter from Darcy to her brother she had managed to pilfer from his office with a compliment on her hosting, a handkerchief he had once given her when she cried at a play – and also items Caroline wished to protect. Moving the Darcy items to the side, Caroline pulled the letters from Elizabeth Bennet to her sister Jane and read them once more, memorizing the details, word-for-word of the plans for Elizabeth and Darcy to travel to London in a week's time.

Chapter Seventeen

Cigar smoke lingered in the foyer of White's Gentlemen's Club on Chesterfield Street as George Wickham worked his charm on the doorkeeper.

"I tell you again, I'm his brother-in-law! Darcy and I grew up together, he is away in the country because his wife is sick, but I am keeping watch on the family house in London with my young wife. She's perfectly lovely, but it's been a bit too many tea parties to talk about society and dresses if you know what I mean, old man. Darcy wouldn't deny me the company of gentlemen, this is merely an oversight."

"I'm most sorry, sir, but you are not listed as one of Mr. Darcy's guests." James Thorpe seethed through his teeth, as he grew tired of this dandy's presence. He knew Mr. Darcy personally, as he was always a great tipper, and to hear this man's claims of marriage to Darcy's younger sister made his blood boil. He would certainly make a note of this to tell Mr. Darcy upon his next visit. "Can you give me your name once more?"

"Wickham. George Wickham. I came here as a youth with old Mr. Darcy. I must be in the guest logs somewhere."

"Mr. Wickham, we don't grant access to the illustrious White's to former guests of members, but to members only. Now, if you can furnish a letter of introduction in your brother-in-law's hand, outlining your privileges in his absence, then our membership committee may consider you a candidate—"

"Bah!" George's frustrations overcame him and he interrupted the doorman's explanation of policy. Darcy would never purposely grant him access to his club. It was time to deploy his alternate plan, with hope that Serendipity would shine on her wayward son once more. Spinning around with a flounce of superiority, George left the club but didn't go far. No, instead of calling for another hack chaise to go back to Darcy House, he casually walked down the lane gripping his new, more stylish cane with his right hand. His ploy paid off as not more than two minutes passed before he physically bumped into an old Cambridge acquaintance.

"I say, watch where you're walking, sir."

George turned back and raised his hat to acknowledge the faux pas and then broke into a wide grin. "Robert! Robert Landry?"

The other man, a few inches shorter than Wickham, and with a touch of ginger to his hair inspected George with slanted eyes of suspicion. "Have we met?"

"It's Georgie! George Wickham!"

Robert's face lit up and George thanked his lucky stars that one of the few men he hadn't owed money to when he was kicked out of Cambridge would cross his path when he needed it most. "Wickham, where have you been hiding yourself? It's been what, six years since we last took a pint together."

"Oh, you wouldn't believe me if I told you the adventures I've had. But now that I'm a married man, I'm settling down and living the quiet life in London." George tapped his cane on the sidewalk a few times to reinforce his jibe.

"The quiet life in London?" Robert laughed at his old friend. "You always have the best stories. Come, have a drink with me at White's, for old times' sake."

George tipped his hat and followed Robert down the same path he had just walked. Robert signed them both in; George flashed James Thorpe a smug smile before climbing the well-worn wooden stairs to the lounge area above.

Two hours later, and Robert Landry well into his cups, George kept up a good disguise of being drunk as well. His eyes flicked numerous times to the two dark haired gentlemen in a far corner with heads bent close together. If he was a betting man, and he was, from the frequent toasts and not so frequent handclasps, the two men had a most interesting scheme afoot.

He nudged Robert and motioned towards the duo, asking if those jolly men should join their own merry party. Without hesitation, Robert stood up and belched to the laughter of the men around them.

"Thomas Stanley! Don't be so dreary in a corner my man, join us in a drink!"

Lord Thomas Stanley, heir to the earldom of Derby frowned and picked up his gloves from the small card table they were using to look over documents. With a nod to his mystery guest, the other man rolled up the parchment between them, which looked to be a ledger of some kind to George's well-trained eye. "You jest Robert to speak of only one drink, from the looks of you. What will that taskmistress of a wife say when you stumble home?" Though sharp tongued, Thomas Stanley, fashioned as Lord Strange, walked over to the haphazard semi-circle of men all drinking beer.

Twitching his nose slightly at the strongly sour odor, Lord Strange ordered a fine wine from the club's man waiting to assist its patrons. As he neared the group, a younger member rose from an armchair to find another place for respite, and Stanley took the better chair without comment.

"Speaking of wives, did you hear this fox plucked the juiciest fruit of Derbyshire before the rest of us knew she was ripe for the taking?" Robert clapped George on the shoulder making him sputter his drink.

Lord Strange's face remained unchanged as he worked out the wife's identity and after a few moments realized there was only one candidate. The youngest sister of his northern neighbor, Fitzwilliam Darcy. "No! Not—"

"The lovely, talented, and small Georgiana Darcy." Wickham flashed his overconfident charmed smile as the men chuckled and repeated his toast to Mrs. Wickham's smallhood.

"How furious was Darcy?"

George shrugged, and then nodded. "Raging like Hades' loss of Persephone."

A Virtue of Marriage

"To the steward's son marrying the master's prime jewel!" Robert raised another toast. The wording annoyed Wickham, but he couldn't play the poor sport now. He reluctantly raised his glass and finished the cup.

Seeing Lord Strange and the mysterious man trade looks, George decided it was now or never to play his hand. Wickham rose and offered a hand to Robert. "It's been a rousing good time, but I must return to my new wife and her delights." This brought yet another loud laugh from the group and they added their own insults to roast Wickham for his damn good luck.

As Wickham started towards the front of the club, the heir of the other half of Derbyshire blocked his path.

"Mr. Wickham, as the Darcy's nearest neighbor, you must join me in a drink to celebrate your nuptials."

Wickham pretended to mull over the invitation, but secretly applauded his perfect timing to illicit just the introduction and invitation he so much desired.

"You are most generous, my Lord. I'm sure my marriage bed will stay warm for another quarter hour or so."

As Lord Thomas Stanley led Wickham back towards the more boisterous group they had drank with before, he took a sharp left away to lead Wickham in the area of the private lounges afforded to the most prestigious members. "How do you like rum?"

Wickham made an involuntary flinch, as rum out in town was typically the most watered down spirit served at the pub. Lord Strange noticed and chuckled. "This bottle, I assure you, is as potent as poison and goes down like honey. My family owns land in the islands and one privilege of the trouble is a cellar stocked with the finest dark rum in all of England."

Stanley's companion poured the drinks and offered a short glass to both. Wickham obliged with a taste as the smooth, dark liquid stung his taste buds before replacing the bark with a pleasant caramel endnote. "Indeed my Lord, you are much mistaken. This is the finest drink in all of England." Wickham smiled and took another deep draft.

As Thomas Stanley sampled his own glass and then closed his eyes in appreciation, he opened them with a new spark behind the bright green irises. "I hate pretense, Mr. Wickham."

Wickham nodded assent, slightly weary this meeting was moving faster than most of his marks.

"My associate, Mr. Bullington, and I have a business proposition for you. The world is changing and mining is the future. I won't let my family languish under my father's misguided rule while he clings to life."

"I was unaware your father was so frail. I hope he isn't ill." Wickham remembered the slight from the Earl of Derby well whenever he visited Pemberley to work with old Mr. Darcy on matters of their shared border to the south.

"You're brash, Wickham. I like that." Lord Strange laughed and his associate joined him for the first time in Wickham's presence.

"My Lord?"

"You speak to the heir of the fifth largest land holdings in the kingdom and hope it is longer before he claims his birthright."

The edge to the greater man's voice made Wickham uneasy, so he opted to enjoy more of his rum and wait for a cue to make his next move.

"Tell me, your marriage settlement must have brought you into quite a small fortune at your sudden disposal. Have you given any thought about how you will invest those funds?" The Viscount ran his ring finger, heavy with the signet of the Stanley family, around the rim of his empty glass. Mr. Bullington offered the bottle to pour more rum, but Thomas waved off with his hand.

Wickham gulped. He wanted the heir of Derby to think he knew nothing about proper investing, to play the perfect patsy. It wasn't difficult to portray since he also knew he had no access to Georgiana's funds. "I have given it a little thought. My brother-in-law of course has his own ideas."

Lord Stanley made another slight movement with his hands and Mr. Bullington unfurled the parchment from earlier.

"These are the profits from the last six months of our operation. You can see that the mine brings a profit of 200% to its investors." Wickham's eyes widened as he read the totals before him in many columns. The names were disguised, Lord A. T.; Lord S. N; Hon. G. K all the way down in the left-most column. "Unfortunately, the recent drought has required some of our landed investors to withdraw their funds, with half of their profits, and we are looking for new investors to help us expand even further into the valley."

Wickham saw the investment totals ranged from £500 to upwards of £10 000 pounds. He needed another drink so he finished off the last of his rum. "How much capital are you gentlemen looking for?"

Lord Strange looked directly on Wickham and held eye contact as he named a figure.

Wickham stood and thanked both men, leaving with assurance that the family lawyers would draft a bank note on the morrow. Lord Strange shook Wickham's hand, as did Mr. Bullington, and they remained in the private lounge room as Wickham headed home.

Pouring them both a fresh glass of rum, Mr. Bullington spoke first. "I thought Darcy was against your plans from the very beginning of building the mine."

"He is. And I doubt very seriously he put Georgiana's dowry in the hands of that man with no strings attached."

"So we won't get the money?"

Thomas Stanley held his glass of rum and drank the entire contents in one swig. "Oh, we'll get the money. That snake would sell his own mother for a taste of riches. We'll have the £2 000 pounds we need to make crabby Cecil Tindrell happy and an extra three for our own coffers. The night, I believe, is ready for more lovelier companionship than White's can offer."

Bullington snatched the fake ledger from the table and rolled it up again. It wouldn't be good for the document to fall into the wrong hands, such as any of the other investors who could add up sums quickly.

Chapter Eighteen

No matter how he ignored it, the tip of Fitzwilliam Darcy's nose grew colder and colder with each moment he scratched quill to paper. Completing a thought in the letter for his Derbyshire steward, the master leaned back and stretched. Exhaling breath he didn't recognize he had been holding, he rose to attend the dwindling coals in the fireplace of the Rosings library. After a warm winter, this sudden cold snap had come from seemingly nowhere and he was surprised to find himself musing that spring most certainly needed to return to her previous position.

Although the study of the late Sir Lewis was available to him, and much easier to regulate temperature-wise, Darcy preferred the open familiarity of his long time refuge. He poked the coals to illicit a brighter effort on their part before lowering and heaving two large logs from the pile into the fray. A few more pokes and readjustments, he was pleased to see feeble flames lick the new additions. He wasn't surprised Lady Catherine never had the fireplaces upgraded to coal burning.

"Darcy, man, I know the situation is dire, but surely you haven't dismissed all of the housemaids already."

Darcy, still crouched near the hearth, turned his head to see his brother in heart, but cousin in fact, standing in the doorway with a smirk on his face. Darcy dusted off his hands, despite their earlier ink stains, and stuck one out to Colonel Richard Fitzwilliam, the second son of the Earl of Matlock, his uncle on his mother's side.

Richard pretended to demure at Darcy's rustic state, before grabbing the man's hand and clasping his forearm in warm greeting. The men silently moved to the sideboard and Darcy poured them each a drink with Richard motioning for just a touch more in his glass. Darcy nodded and obliged.

Settling into the two chairs near the fire, Darcy swirled the thick liquid in his glass and watched the reflection of flames in the glass rim.

"I did not dismiss all of the housemaids, not that Aunt Catherine would sustain such a purge. I merely weighed the consequences of waiting for assistance over the state of my cold nose and decided the strongest course of action was to rectify the situation myself."

"Hear, hear, the master decided and acted." Richard gulped a large swig down after raising his glass in mockery.

To those who didn't know the master of Pemberley and Rosings well, his stony expression would appear to be one of censure. But Richard saw the twinkle in his cousin's eye, not that Darcy's reception ever diminished his desire to tease.

Darcy matched Richard with an equally large gulp, just as a maid entered with a curtsy at the door. He motioned with his fingers for her to approach, and she handed him a simple folded note, before curtsying and leaving the room.

Darcy flipped the missive open:

Cousin-

It is not in my habit to make silly requests as a woman on her deathbed, but my friend, Mrs. Collins, has not visited in two days. Please make inquiries if there are any means we could assist her in returning? Her company and reading is a small light in the darkness I am facing.

Anne

Without much interest, Darcy commanded the note to the flames and returned to his chair. He mulled Anne's request and tried to weigh how controlled he would be to visit the parsonage. The Archbishop was to arrive in just three more days and while difficult, he had managed to endure not seeing his Elizabeth in that time.

"You are frowning. A penny for your thoughts?"

"Do you have such penny to pay?" Darcy said dryly, not above his own manner of provoking Richard's ire.

"Two! But come; come what note has you so out of sorts? Has Aunt planned venison pie for dinner?"

That venison pie was the least favorite of Darcy's was a well-known family fact, after a disastrous time of him running from the dinner table at the age of ten when his mother and father attempted to make him eat it. Since that thrashing for poor manners, Darcy no longer ran from any unpalatable meal, but limited such cuisine to three drawn out mouthfuls and no more.

"Anne worries that Mrs. Collins has not been to visit her in a few days and she has requested I inquire into the matter." Darcy took a final drink from his glass before rising to refill his and take Richard's to do the same.

"So you would deny a dying woman her harmless request?"

"It's not that light of a decision. She is asking me to tell the parson to send his wife for your future wife's comfort."

"And that is not within the realm of work for a parson?" Richard said more as a statement of irony than as a question.

Darcy frowned further and returned with fresh beverages. He took a deep breath and resolved that as always, he would hold his own control and not let his passionate affections shake him. It would be wonderful to see Elizabeth and inhale her delicate lavender scent.

"Alright Richard, you have persuaded me. Let's saddle our horses and ride to the parsonage."

"Wait, I must go as well? This sounds to be estate business." Richard hoped for a private audience with Anne while Darcy was gone.

Darcy finally gave his cousin an elusive smile. "As the chief proponent of the scheme, it seems only fitting you see it through. Unless His Majesty's Finest is fearful of a lowly parson…," Darcy said, trailing off and collecting his post from the desk to drop off in town. Richard had yet to fully appreciate the idiocy of Mr. Collins since their last visit was cut short.

"Afraid of a parson? I should think not."

Darcy returned his inkwell and quill to its rightful drawer. "Oh, somehow I think you will find this parson quite extraordinary."

Chapter Nineteen

Once saddled, Sampson and Alexander, two chestnut hunters sharing the same sire, took to their normal race past the post and across the meadow separating Rosings and Hunsford. After a last rousing gallop over the hill, both Darcy and Colonel Fitzwilliam slowed their horses to navigate the narrowing path to the parsonage. Darcy ducked his head slightly to avoid an overgrown branch, as the gravel road was a barely wide enough for a phaeton, and not two strapping stallions traveling side-by-side.

"Have you considered a celebration for Georgiana's birthday?"

Darcy clicked his tongue and pulled on his reins slightly to keep Alexander alert. "I have sent my sister a new collection of music books and a few inexpensive pieces of my mother's jewels. Reset of course, in the latest fashions."

Colonel Fitzwilliam pulled back on Sampson to let Darcy cross a small footbridge first. The wider road was more than two hundred yards to their right with a bridge over the same creek wide enough for two carts. The bridge was an improvement he and Darcy oversaw final construction on last spring. The staff at Rosings, for a shorter walk to church and market, used this crossing.

"Will she not expect a ball or some other type celebration?"

"You are jesting. I will not reward her headstrong, impertinent decision to tie us to that ... man ... for all of our days. Could you attend such an event with him?" After a moment's pause, Darcy added the last argument against a party for Georgiana. "As her husband, the provenance of planning and paying for such a fete now rests on his happy shoulders."

Colonel Fitzwilliam let the discussion drop and both men dismounted and tied their companions' reins to nearby tree.

Briskly knocking on the door, Darcy finally took a moment to take in the improvements on the parson's cottage his aunt oversaw last year as well. The stonework appeared patched in the places needed, and a new coat of blue paint covered the shutters. The side garden was new to him and he wondered if it was the chief work of Charlotte Collins or the result of austerity measures.

After such a long delay, Darcy looked to Colonel Fitzwilliam as he knocked again, louder and with more urgency. Seconds later, Mr. Collins himself opened the door.

"Gentlemen, forgive me, I was in my study contemplating this week's sermon as the Archbishop shall be present. What brings you to call at my humble abode? Though your mere presence elevates the home, yet on days without your gracious visit I am most pleased with the dwelling furnished by the generous living provided by the most charitable Lady Catherine. I trust that your aunt is in good health?"

Darcy broke his normal austere facade to glance at Colonel Fitzwilliam's slacking jaw. At catching his cousin's eye, Colonel Fitzwilliam closed his mouth and barely hid his smile at the parson's introduction.

"Mr. Collins, may I formally introduce you to my cousin, Colonel Richard Fitzwilliam?" Darcy exposed the ridiculous man's false closeness to him and his cousin through Lady Catherine's long-winded speeches about her nephews. There had been no time for a proper introduction the last time they met due to Anne's health.

"How do you do?" The colonel made a pert nod to the lowly parson, now cowering slightly from his earlier and typical faux pas.

"Colonel Fitzwilliam, it is an honor to meet the illustrious nephew of my patroness."

"On the subject of our mutual aunt, she is in fine health. It is my cousin we call on you about." Colonel Fitzwilliam's easy manners saved Darcy from the trouble of addressing Collin's obsession with Lady Catherine and her whims.

"Ah, poor Miss de Bourgh. Is her time so very near? Is this a summons to Rosings so I may serve the family in its time of great spiritual need?"

Darcy took a moment to glance at their horses to ensure they were sufficiently restrained. "Perhaps we might discuss this in a less public location than your front door stoop, Mr. Collins?"

Collins took a look inside his own house with a nervous, barely observable quibble to his lower lip. He opened the door wider to allow the two gentlemen entryway. "Of course, please join me in my study."

As the three walked back towards the parson's study, their boots and heavier weight making a mighty echo on the wooden floor of the home, Collins offered them both the refreshment of tea.

"I'll take something stronger if you have it." Ever the one to make a situation jolly, Colonel Fitzwilliam clapped the squat parson on his right shoulder. The force of the unexpected blow made Collins nearly jump in reaction. Standing with his feet perfectly together, the man of the cloth nearly shrank in the broad physique of His Majesty's Finest. A reluctant host, Collins poured the Colonel a drink of his best cognac, and offered the same to Mr. Darcy, who declined.

"Please, have a seat." Collins motioned as he took his normal seat behind a humble writing desk that appeared to be designed for a woman it was so small in stature. "I fear this must be extremely difficult for a man of such exalted status as you, Mr. Darcy, but it is with the utmost discretion that I will now hear your troubles and upon on my honor, as a servant of our Lord and Savior, ease your conscience in any manner available."

Darcy inhaled and moved to the very edge of his seat, almost leering at the pompous parson. "I see you are engaged in a great deal of work, we must be a complete intrusion. Forgive me."

Darcy placed a hand on his right knee, a long-standing sign between the two of them for Richard to wait and play along. His eyes flicked to his right to see if Richard noticed and a slight nod from his cousin was all Darcy needed to see.

"I am flattered that you noticed so, sir. Yes, it is a most busy time for the church and me. We are repairing the damage done to the roof over the winter and I've received word that Bishop Lowell is to also grace us with his visit in two months' time to inspect the rectory and parish. I am also overseeing the spring planting–"

"And Mrs. Collins I take it is assisting you in visiting the glebe land families and tending to the sick."

Mr. Collins was startled at the interruption, but recovered quickly.

"Ah, I've lessened the demands that my office might impose on Mrs. Collins. She assures me she supports my work and families we are to care for most fervently with prayer and careful reflection."

Mr. Darcy raised an eyebrow at this description of Charlotte, but would never presume to call her undevoted to their Heavenly Father.

"You don't plan to visit your mutual relations in Hertfordshire in the coming weeks as part of the customary traveling season?" Darcy assumed Collins had no idea of his plans with Elizabeth and might intend to return his cousin to her family in Hertfordshire. He may not know of the breach.

Mr. Collins sat baffled for a moment that Mr. Darcy was so interested in his business, but at the same time, completely disinterested as to interrupt him. He hesitated a moment before answering. "No, I believe my wife and I visited extensively during our courtship and during the time leading up to our happy nuptials. My cousin has managed those lands for decades and would not take kindly to my interfering at this juncture, even though I am the heir to Longbourn." Collins sniffed and raised his chin a bit, as Richard struggled not to laugh.

Taking a more relaxed posture in his chair, Mr. Darcy paused at the mention of Mr. Collins' marriage. Removing his hands to meet at his navel in an interlaced fashion, Colonel Fitzwilliam took this as his cue to speak up.

"Mr. Collins, my cousin and I are in need of your services via your wife. Miss de Bourgh's weakness has increased and the rattling in her cough is most haunting. Seeing what I've seen of Death on the battlefield, it is too short a time before we must say farewell to Anne for my tastes. She is never one to complain or make grandiose requests." Colonel Fitzwilliam politely swallowed more of the foul tasting cognac for propriety's sake, but made a note to never ask persons of lower annual salary than even he for a good drink.

"No, Lady Catherine's daughter is the picture of humility and discretion that we might all strive to don as our time to meet our Maker draws near. The world will indeed be short one of the brightest gems in society when we lose Miss Anne de Bourgh." Mr. Collins speech patterns returned to his practiced monotony of a pulpit recitation.

"Then you will agree most heartily with our plan to install Mrs. Collins and her friend visiting, Miss Elizabeth Bennet, in one of the guest wings to keep vigil over Anne in her last days, as she has requested!" Colonel Fitzwilliam's grin maintained its position despite Mr. Collins' souring facial expression.

"No, gentlemen, I cannot acquiesce to this request. The most wise Lady Catherine has cautioned me about undue exposure of my cousin's spirited nature to Miss be Bourgh at this time when her mortal soul is most in danger to secure salvation."

"Of all the preposterous –" Mr. Darcy rose violently from his chair. "You sit there, sir, and question the salvation of MY cousin?"

Mr. Collin's face paled under the ire of Mr. Darcy. "No, of course not. Miss de Bourgh is the epitome of grace and charity, and would sooner fly with angels than anyone of my acquaintance. But Mrs. Collins is having difficulty adjusting to the calling of a parson's wife, and she would be a poor influence at this time, I believe."

"How can you charge such behavior of your own wife?" Colonel Fitzwilliam was appalled by the nature this conversation was taking in discussing a woman he had yet to meet. "Or is this a delusion my aunt has pressed upon you?"

Mr. Collins glanced back and forth at both gentlemen with an expression of complete shock. He stood to match Darcy's position. "You declare Lady Catherine to suffer from delusions, not on my word!"

"Settle down, Mr. Collins. No, Aunt Catherine doesn't suffer from delusions in the strictest sense, but knowing her all of my life, her suppositions of others' behavior are trumped to the most extreme description on the slightest provocation. Why I myself am a loafing drunkard, unfit for the most elegant of dinner tables." Colonel Fitzwilliam lifted the last of the cognac in mock toast and knocked it back.

"Richard, you are a loafing drunkard to those whom you do not wish to know your true nature." Mr. Darcy quipped.

"Fair enough, Cousin, but if my true gentle disposition were known in the Army, I'd have a difficult time prying intelligence for my superiors' ears."

Mr. Collins gulped as he sat once more before two men who clearly outclassed him. Still, as her husband, he had the right to deny Charlotte and his cousin from this visit, and save his own skin with Lady Catherine in the process. After all, she was his patroness and he had worked under her tutelage for three years with a clear understanding of her expectations for loyalty and obedience.

"I cannot grant your request to send Mrs. Collins and my cousin to Rosings. I fear Elizabeth's behavior will be disreputable for the society Lady Catherine is accustomed to encountering. Her father had a loose hand with her upbringing, and I am working earnestly to guide my cousin in the ways and manners now expected of her lower rank."

"Lower rank? Is not Miss Bennet the daughter of a gentleman and thus the same rank of cousin and myself? Are you not to inherit that same property, thus soon to join the same rank?" Darcy chose not to address the work Mr. Collins might be doing to guide Elizabeth's manners to be more like his own crude posturings. Though he had to admit, having met the younger Bennet sisters, he couldn't completely fault Mr. Collins for his opinion of Mr. Bennet.

Mr. Collins blanched. His own father, a third son, never owned land out of an inability to manage funds. This made Oxford nearly unbearable and the chief reason why Collins pursued a living with great focus. The law and military were far too competitive for his tastes.

Lucky enough to complete university on the generosity of his late grandmother's will, Beatrice Collins was a daughter of a wealthy baronet in Matlock, before she married the second son of a neighbor wealthy from trade with the colonies. Lady Catherine remembered Beatrice as an older woman invited to help accustom Lady Anne and herself in the arts of polite conversation, long before Beatrice married Henry William Collins. In accepting his grandmother's inheritance, as she had outlived her husband by twenty years, he himself had taken on the honorable name of Collins and cast aside the underachieving name of Bennet with glee.

"Be that as it may, my wife is not at home presently. She is out on an errand with our cook and my cousin." Mr. Collins smiled smugly as he lied through his teeth to the two men before him. He knew both were locked in their rooms for disobeying his express orders to no longer give food and assistance to the heathen family on his lands. He had not wished to strike Elizabeth so hard, but her chit of a reply that the candlesticks somehow did not belong to him since they were a wedding gift from her aunt and uncle was an impertinence he would not tolerate.

Mr. Darcy realized this was going to get them nowhere and began to move towards the door when a large thump could be heard upstairs. All three men looked up at the ceiling.

"Sir, perhaps your wife returned early without your knowledge?" Colonel Fitzwilliam found the blood draining from Mr. Collins face a curious reaction indeed.

"Err, yes, she did return but a few moments before your arrival. I had forgotten she had retired to rest."

"Good God man, that was a nasty crash. Perhaps you should check to see that she is alright?" Mr. Darcy prodded the man, putting Mr. Collins in a completely stuck position.

"Yes, I shall do just that." Without thinking, Mr. Collins fumbled with his top desk drawer to pull out the key. Neither man missed the implications, though where Colonel Fitzwilliam was able to steel his gaze as indifferent, Mr. Darcy's eyes widened and then slanted in rage.

Both Fitzwilliam men waited at the bottom of the stairs as they heard Mr. Collins speak to Charlotte and Elizabeth just upstairs and alert them that Miss de Bourgh's time was near. Despite trying to dissuade their visit at this moment, but thinking they might go in a few days, Elizabeth informed her cousin that Miss de Bourgh may not have a few days and her regrets would be too great.

She almost pushed her oaf of a cousin aside to descend the stairs in a glory only the most noble of women pull off. With a glint of defiance in her eyes, she donned her bonnet and gloves as both Rosings men took shocking stock of the large, grayish purple mark across her right cheek. Charlotte followed in silence, as if trying to hide she was siding against her husband.

With a smile, she turned to her cousin, now on the ground floor with them. "Don't worry Cousin Collins, I am sure Dr. Smeads can attend to this nasty gash from my foolhardiness. I must be careful not to slip on one of my garments and fall into the bedside table again."

Mr. Collins gulped, as the two men nearly a head taller than him both moved a protective step closer to Elizabeth. The tension in the air caused the ladies hold their breath. "Er . . . yes, I'm certain Lady Catherine will be most eager to share her generosity by instructing Dr. Smeads to do just that. As soon as I finish my work here, I will join you at Rosings to attend her Ladyship in this dark, dark time."

Chapter Twenty

The odd foursome walked the short distance back to Rosings across one of Elizabeth's favorite meadows. She knew she should be self conscious about the mark on her cheek, but the glorious sunshine and smells of fresh greenery invigorated her spirit with each step.

"Miss Bennet, forgive me for appearing bold, but you have a quick step!" Colonel Fitzwilliam emanated his normal charm, as Elizabeth was a good two or three paces ahead of the gentlemen. She smiled broadly in response.

"No offense taken, Colonel. I am known as a great walker and it has been some days for me to stretch my legs. It is we who should worry to offend as our presence forces you gentlemen to walk your gorgeous companions when you are clearly more accustomed to riding them."

"Do you ride?" Darcy blurted out, realizing it was a strange question to ask of his Elizabeth, but he also could not recall discussing the matter with her. Darcy felt better when he remembered he had to keep up appearances about not knowing Miss Bennet that well, though his blood boiled over that parson! He wanted to march back and throttle the man.

Elizabeth shook her head. "Sadly, not well I'm afraid. We only had two horses on our lands and they were mostly reserved for work or when Papa had to go into town for provisions. We did have a pony for a time, but a cruel winter stole her life when I was but eleven."

The mention of the unfortunate beast's fate brought back a mood of somberness as they came to the grand mansion. Charlotte casually made her way to the door, removed her bonnet and gloves and began to walk towards the back hall where the servant's staircase was housed. Darcy and Richard exchanged a look before the Colonel called out to her.

"Mrs. Collins, I believe the shortest walk to Mrs. Darcy resides this way," and he pointed up the stairs.

Charlotte nodded meekly; embarrassed she was now instructed to take the main staircase as opposed to the instructions Lady Catherine had laid down for her once daily visits to the ailing Anne. Elizabeth joined her in taking the stairs, resisting the urge to glance down at Mr. Darcy one more time. Before Darcy could follow the ladies up the stairs, Colonel Fitzwilliam clapped Darcy's shoulder.

"Let's make sure our beasts of burden are well groomed, Darce, before we visit our cousin."

Darcy glared at his cousin with his back to the ladies. Their horses were always well tended at Rosings, Darcy made sure of it. But he knew Richard must have a thought on his mind and needed a private word.

As the two men stepped out into the sunshine once more, Darcy didn't have to wait long.

"Did you see the bruise on her cheek, cousin? What could a nice lady like her be doing with a mark on her such as that? Her story of falling today doesn't explain the deep purple and indigo colors. That injury is at least a day or two old!"

Darcy scowled, remembering the sight of Elizabeth's face as she came down the stairs to join them.

"I shall have a strongly worded conversation with that parson of mine."

"Oho, will you now? And what shall you say to him? Inform the man on how he must treat his female cousin in his protection?"

Darcy glanced about to see if any servants might have overheard as they neared the stables. He realized it would overstep his place to interfere in another man's household over a woman so officially wholly unconnected to himself.

"It is abominable for a man to raise a hand to a woman," he hissed.

"We must not jeopardize our plans. Your lady is made of stern stuff, that much I can say. Did you see the way she stared him down before we left? Have faith, Darce, she will be safe."

Darcy stopped walking. Richard's assessment stung him and he immediately panicked over what further injury she might endure.

Darcy glared at Richard's sympathy with a jealous lover's eye "It was dangerous to bring her here."

"You were insistent."

"I said no such thing!"

Richard made a mock face of surprise. "Truly? All that whining of being separated must have been a different man's letters I read each week."

"Richard. Collins is the man she was to marry. I've told you . . ."

Richard kicked a pebble and frowned. "Well, we're in a fine pickle now! The lot of us. It's a damned morbid comedy, that's what it is."

Angry and annoyed, Darcy turned on his heel and strode to the house. Let Richard pamper the horses, he was going to see to his future wife, and her friend, and make sure they had every comfort.

As Darcy entered the sitting room outside of Anne's bedroom, he could hear Elizabeth's voice through the cracked doorway. Taking a deep breath, he acknowledged that eavesdropping once again was reprehensible, but he couldn't deny himself the pleasure of drinking in her voice. He closed his eyes and listened, but snapped them back open as he quickly realized the subject matter the three women were discussing. At that point, he was rooted to the spot to hear more.

"It was horrific, Anne. That poor family needs Christian charity, not exile! So yes, I sold the candlesticks and gave Diana the money. It took Collins two days to notice there were wooden ones on the table."

"Was he most upset that you had helped the family he was evicting or that the candlesticks were gone?"

Both women laughed leaving Anne confused.

"See, I knew you would help me see the folly in this! I think it might have been losing the precious silver candlesticks, that was the biggest blow."

As the laughter stopped, Anne's voice became serious.

"But he struck you, you must be careful, Miss Bennet."

"Oh it doesn't hurt now. And better me than Charlotte, though I'm certain he has struck her before, has he not?" Elizabeth looked to her friend who hid her face in silent shame by looking down.

"Yes, but" Anne stopped to catch her breath and refused her friend Charlotte's assistance. Once she could slowly breathe in normally, she continued, "But next time he might not just leave it at one strike. Promise me, promise me you will take care to not raise his ire. Not before the Archbishop arrives."

Elizabeth took a deep breath and paused as she thought she saw movement in Miss de Bourgh's sitting room. As she took a few steps closer and opened the bedroom door wider, she saw an empty room. Shrugging, she turned back to her friend and resolved to move to a happier subject. She meant to ask Anne about the dreams and wishes she had before she became ill.

Chapter Twenty-One

Darcy took the stairs two at a time. He scared a footman about to cross the foyer with his sudden arrival causing the young man to immediately turn and go back the way he came. Darcy was outside and about to march back across the meadow between Rosings and Hunsford when Richard called out to him. This broke the spell of rage Darcy was under and allowed him to bellow.

"He struck her! The coward hit her face because she helped a tenant family!"

Richard swiftly moved to stand in front of Darcy and coaxed him back towards the house. "We knew he hit her, there was no question about that and we agreed there could never be a cause.

Now, come with me to the library. Let's have a drink and be reasonable."

"Reasonable? Reasonable? That man deserves to be beat within an inch of his life!"

"And what would that achieve? How would marching over there to teach that windbag a lesson help Mrs. Collins? Will it make a man like him less likely to strike out or more likely to prove he's in control? THINK man. Better yet, will it help us marry our loves or potentially send your Elizabeth packing this very afternoon?"

Richard had said the magic word. Darcy blew his frustrations out and ruffled his own hair in the aggravation of feeling powerless. It was not an emotion he was accustomed to experiencing.

"I need a drink."

Richard grinned and followed Darcy back inside. "Yes, and we're raiding the finest. I need to wash that horse's piss the Parson calls brandy out of my system."

The men were surprised to discover Elizabeth in their retreat of choice, reaching far above her head to a dusty shelf in the corner. Richard rushed forward to assist her. As she pointed to the tome she needed, she collected the other thick volume she had already pulled down on her own and began walking towards Darcy with a wide smile. Darcy wasted no time in pouring himself and Richard a stiff drink, and downed his in a swallow before facing the beautiful, yet flawed, visage before him.

"Mr. Darcy? Colonel?" Elizabeth looked over her shoulder to beckon her book boy to bring his burden to the front of the room. "I must enlist your aid in making mischief."

"Mischief, Miss Bennet?" Darcy hoped if he forced himself to keep using her polite name, it would help him to put his emotions back into their cold reserve. "To what end is this mischief?"

"Why pleasing Anne!" Elizabeth beamed at the two men; clearly satisfied she would not be denied. "I propose we read, nay perform, as much as we can, A Midsummer Night's Dream for Anne, I mean Miss de Bourgh, as she has just told me that one play she wished she had been afforded the opportunity to see was the same."

Darcy poured himself another drink as a memory flooded his mind, of a young Anne, nearly eleven, laughing at Richard and himself trying to wage a proper naval battle in the small pond on the west side of the property. She was healthy that year, before a bout with pneumonia that winter would rob her of every ounce of youth and send her into a faded presence. She had splashed water with her hand to make waves, causing both Richard and himself to cry out, to which she had explained surely even in battle, Mother Nature had her say. She had been reading a collection of Shakespeare's works that summer, the gold-leafed volume Sir Lewis had given her for her birthday.

"I think it's a splendid idea, what say you Darcy?"

Darcy cleared his throat. "Of course, anything for Anne."

Chapter Twenty-Two

The servants of Darcy House in London disproved of the former Miss Darcy and her husband, but nothing rankled Mrs. Potter more than the mischief she saw afoot at this moment. Strangers of ill repute visited the home on a near daily basis and more and more items were missing. She had not proof yet, but something strange was going on and she was determined to get to the bottom of it!

After dismissing two young maids to see to the guest rooms, Mrs. Potter bustled her way to the master's study full of vim and vigor. That imposter George Wickham should not take her Master's place, but she was powerless to tell him otherwise, even if she did find it repulsive. After knocking on the door and entering, the man sat oblivious to all behind her Master's desk with papers and letters all around.

"What is it? I'm a very busy man and cannot—" Mr. Wickham looked up and his expression immediately shifted to disappointment to see Mrs. Potter. The older lady crossed her arms at his sudden change in demeanor, knowing too well he hoped her to be a young maid for an afternoon dalliance. Never in her years of service at this house had she sent a maid packing to her family, and she just did such a week ago due to this man's snake.

"Begging your pardon, sir, but the vase in the library, the blue Ming? It be missing, sir."

"I'm sure Mrs. Wickham ordered it cleaned or packed away. She is changing the decor and has requested some items from Pemberley. I expect they shall arrive today."

"Pemberley?" Mrs. Potter's voiced failed her for a moment. These leeches were to plunder the spoils of Pemberley as well? She must write to Mr. Darcy and Mrs. Reynolds straight away!

"Is there a problem with my wife decorating her home?" George Wickham glared at the housekeeper with a wild look in his eye.

"No, of course not, sir. Mrs. Wickham has excellent taste and I'm certain when the Master returns, he will be most pleased with his sister's efforts." Mrs. Potter remained indifferent in her expression though she felt enormous triumph inside as she managed to remind the pretender of who truly owned this home.

"I'm certain you have work to do, leave me to mine." Wickham dismissed the housekeeper with a wave of his hand. He could not be bothered with some lowly servant needing to understand his plans. As Wickham tallied the sums again and again, even with the money he would get for the statues and artwork from Pemberley, he was still five hundred quid short. Lord Strange and Mr. Bullington did not appear to be men of an understanding nature when a business associate failed to fulfill an obligation. Wickham was going to have to find the last of the money somewhere.

Leaning back in the chair of Fitzwilliam Darcy, George Wickham dreamed of the freedom only wealth could provide. This one investment, a small portion of Georgiana's dowry if he had possession of it as was his right as her husband, stood as the best path to his future of fancy-free living. Wickham cursed Darcy and snapped forward to bang his fist on the desk. That man always thwarted his plans at every turn!

Spying a miniature of his lovely wife on the desk, Wickham's lips began to curl in a sinister grin. Perhaps there was one asset he had

A Virtue of Marriage

overlooked, one of great value. Picking up the small portrait of a thirteen-year-old Georgiana, he felt especially light as his own loins responded to the picture. She wouldn't like it, but if he charmed her enough, George had no doubt he would find a very compliant wife to his wishes and that of his friends with money to pay for her attentions.

Chapter Twenty-Three

Colonel Fitzwilliam lay stiff as a board on the cream carpeted floor in Anne Darcy's bedroom and Fitzwilliam Darcy held the hands of Elizabeth Bennet close to his chest.

"I had no judgment when to her I swore!" Darcy stared into Elizabeth's eyes, holding his part of Lysander, not needing much motivation to evoke a desperate man.

"Nor none, in my mind, now that you give her o'er." Elizabeth attempted to pull her hands away but Darcy held them fiercely, just as he'd seen done on the London stage. Anne grinned from ear to ear watching the scene unfold, pressing her hands together and rising to sit higher than her fluffed pillows would allow.

Charlotte Collins sat next to her, riveted by the emotional tension in the room. If she had not known her friend to be a gentlewoman, she might have wondered if Mr. Darcy and the Colonel had hired a professional actress from London for the fete.

"Demetrius loves her, and he loves not you." Again, Darcy looked into Elizabeth's eyes but noticed a small smile creeping on her lips. He looked down to see what was the source of her amusement when a stifled snore came from near his feet. Exasperated, Darcy nudged the lifeless body of his cousin Richard with his foot with more force than was polite.

Richard flailed his arms at an unknown assailant, managing to knock Darcy's tall legs from under him by catching him right at the knees, which pulled Elizabeth Bennet down onto a heap with both men on the floor.

"Richard, you dolt!"

Richard was fully awake now that the weight of two persons had landed on his gut and he was quickly pushing both away from him. Elizabeth landed soundly on her rear end straight onto the floor, causing her to burst out laughing.

"How could you fall asleep?"

"What? I'm a soldier old man, and this floor is one of the most comfortable ones I've had a pleasure to lie on." Richard pretended to readjust himself to resume slumbering.

"Oh Richard, have you truly slept on many floors?" Anne asked, barely above a whisper.

Richard opened his eyes and winked, before closing them again. Taking a deep breath, he quickly rose and began shouting in a bombastic voice:

"O Helena, goddess, nymph, perfect, divine!" The Colonel reached down to help Elizabeth up as she was still trying to remain serious. She continued her giggles as Richard forgot most of his speech and instead gave her a flourished bow and kissed her hand.

Deciding that would have to do, Elizabeth pulled her much abused hands away from the second gentleman to claim them this afternoon, in the spirit of the dramatic arts, and placed them on her hips.

"O spite! O hell! I see you all are bent to set against me for your merriment:" She wagged her finger at both men, and glanced to Anne and Charlotte, both ladies were watching her little play with rapt attention. Elizabeth took a moment to begin pacing between the two men and raised her voice a notch in admonishment.

"If you were civil and knew courtesy," she paused and took the opportunity to offer a hand

A Virtue of Marriage

to Mr. Darcy who had taken a casual reclining position of the floor with his arms resting on his knees after the spill of three, emphasizing the words she was speaking. "You would not do me thus much injury."

"And the same could be said of you, Miss Bennet!" barked a voice none of them wished to hear from the doorway.

The smile on Darcy's face disappeared as he dropped Elizabeth's hand and stepped between his aunt and her prey.

"Aunt, might we employ you to play the part of Titania, Queen of the Fairies?"

"Fairies! I should think not!"

"Mr. Collins, we could use you as Nick Bottom, a most crucial part in the play!" Richard called out, spying the toad of a parson hiding behind his aunt's wide girth just inside Anne's attached sitting room.

Mr. Collins absently took a step forward at the invitation, only to receive the fiercest glare from his patroness. "Er, while the invitation is most inviting, I fear at this moment I am not inclined to dramatic displays as befitting the tastes and culture of those present."

"It's Miss de Bourgh's favorite play, but she's never seen it performed. We are acting as a kindness to her." Elizabeth hurried to add, biting her tongue at Richard assigning her cousin the role of the ass.

"Of course she hasn't seen it performed, her health has precluded her from such energetic and emotional influences, Miss Bennet. Had she been of stout health, she would have been a most celebrated admirer of the theater and a patron of the finest plays!" Anne's mother was not to be swayed.

"You take exception, madam, that I fulfill a dying wish of my future wife?" Mr. Darcy's voice resumed an icy tone he reserved only for his aunt, especially for occasions where she forgot her soon-to-be status as the Dowager of Rosings, not the Mistress.

"Darcy, you risk her health!"

"No, Momma, they are making me laugh!" Anne said loudly, holding the hands of Mrs. Collins sitting next to her on the bed.

Lady Catherine took one more calculated look at the room before her, disapproving of the levity and gaiety for a sickroom. "Well then."

She turned around to make like she was going to leave, causing Elizabeth to release the breath she hadn't realized she was holding.

"Mr. Collins," she called, and glanced over her shoulder to the squat man looking back and forth at Mr. Darcy and herself "weren't you just telling me how you were thinking Mrs. Collins should rest before dinner?"

"Why, why yes, Lady Catherine, you had just finished telling me how concerned you were for her and Cousin Elizabeth's welfare given the devotion they both have bestowed upon Miss de Bourgh. It would not due to have three ladies ill, it is best they all rest as you say, and you are most generous to offer them rooms to do so." The irony of Mr. Collins trumpeting Lady Catherine's generosity was punctuated by a deep rumble and harsh crash of thunder thanks to a spring storm. Three hours ago it was decided that the Hunsford party would dine and stay at Rosings overnight, as the weather was too harsh for them to return.

Elizabeth rolled her eyes involuntarily. She looked to Anne and slightly shook her head to confirm to the woman she was no burden. Anne gave a feeble smile and pressed her lips together, which Elizabeth recognized as her way of stifling a coughing fit. Taking a deep breath, Elizabeth pushed past Mr. Darcy and took her cousin's arm.

"Perhaps we have given Miss de Bourgh too much excitement for her condition and can wait to continue the play." Before the Collinses could follow Lady Catherine out of Anne's suite, Lady Catherine turned around and eyed the young woman most carefully. But Elizabeth didn't flinch. "Tomorrow," she said, with a light air to her words.

Once in the hall, Elizabeth immediately broke from her cousin's arm to return to the guest chamber she was assigned earlier in the day.

"Miss Bennet," Lady Catherine called before taking the main staircase back to her parlor.

Elizabeth turned and curtsied with her head bowed, before rising to look at the old woman. "Yes, Lady Catherine?"

"We are dining at 7 o'clock sharp. I expect you to take your meal in my dining room, not with my daughter."

"Yes, ma'am, as you please." Elizabeth bowed her head to hide her frown. She had underestimated Lady Catherine's intelligence, as Elizabeth had planned to take her dinner with Anne.

"Please do what you can with your hair to hide the ghastly mark on your cheek. You shouldn't display your clumsiness in front of my nephews."

Curtsying once more, Elizabeth turned to continue her trek to the beautiful yellow-papered room made up for her disposal and a copy of Shakespeare's plays on her nightstand. If she could not perform, she would rehearse her lines, as they would certainly be replaying today's scene after the disaster of Colonel Fitzwilliam falling asleep and Lady Catherine barging in. She looked over her shoulder to see if Mr. Collins was following her, but instead flooded with relief to see her cousin had followed Lady Catherine, with Charlotte in tow, downstairs to tend to more of the madwoman's whims.

No more than a few moments passed in the sanctuary of her guest room than she heard a knock at her door. She opened it expecting Harriet, Miss de Bourgh's maid, only to see Mr. Darcy standing before her.

"Mr. Darcy." Elizabeth immediately dropped into a curtsy.

"Miss Bennet." He perfunctory bowed, then stood there in silence.

"Can I assist you in some way, sir?" Elizabeth's last words of her question faded away as the man simply stepped into her bedroom and took command of the door handle from her. The impropriety of what they were both tacitly agreeing to do made her thrilled and nervous at the same time.

"I heard you."

Elizabeth took a few steps away from her secretly betrothed to maintain space and calm, then looked at him with her eyebrow arched. "Sir, I did not say a word since entering this room, I assure you."

"No, before. With Anne. I heard you."

Elizabeth pressed her lips together and clasped her hands in front of her. She didn't know what to say. Was Fitzwilliam angry she sold the candlesticks? Would he find her to be in the wrong as well? Her silence prompted Mr. Darcy to add to his earlier confession.

"I should not have been listening, truly. It's just that, your injury, and where you were when we collected you…"

"Why are you bringing up my embarrassment?"

"Your embarrassment? YOUR embarrassment? It should be HIS embarrassment!"

"Please, keep your voice down."

Darcy frowned. He took a breath and tugged on his left coat sleeve with his other hand. "I apologize, my temper got the better of me."

Elizabeth furrowed her brow for a moment and then looked back at Mr. Darcy. "Have you heard of the Holbein family?"

Darcy frowned again. "You misunderstand me, Miss Bennet —- wait, what does my driver have to do with this?"

"Your driver?"

"Yes, Peter Holbein, his family has been in my family's employ for three generations."

Elizabeth felt delighted and could not help herself from giddily jumping up and down. "Of course! The uncle! Your driver's brother I believe is a tenant on Mr. Collins' land. Only Mr. Collins has plans to run them off, because they are practicing Catholics, and the father has a broken back which made small Peter steal eggs . . ."

"Wait, I don't follow what you mean. Are you saying you sold the candlesticks to provide money for relations of my driver?"

Elizabeth nodded.

"But you stole Mr. Collins' property!"

Elizabeth shook her head, and bit her lip.

"Elizabeth?"

"I didn't so much sell the candlesticks as let Charlotte think I did. I had some money from my uncle, enough to satisfy one quarter's rent so the family is no longer in arrears, but if you, sir, could aid me, we could protect the entire Holbein family from eviction. That's what made Mr. Collins angry. When he said he would still evict the family, I could not abide such horrific treatment for those innocent children. They are hungry, Fitzwilliam."

Elizabeth's words pained Darcy's heart. How could any family be allowed to suffer on his aunt's lands, albeit lands under the parsonage's control? It was not to be borne! Darcy's mind reeled from the mess Elizabeth laid before him, another complication in his already complicated existence, but he was not cross with her for bringing the problem to him. He only wished she had done so in the first place rather than trying to manage the problem on her own and bearing the violence of that parson in return.

"Have I angered you, sir?" Elizabeth watched the stormy expressions on her Fitzwilliam's face and her stomach now pained her in response. The turmoil in her heart tumbled relentlessly in her gut.

Darcy closed the distance between them and pulled her into an embrace. "I was ready to kill him, with my own bare hands. Richard stopped me. Said you were strong."

"Your cousin is a wise man." Elizabeth giggled as her nose tickled against his shirt. She tried to pull back, but he would not release her.

"I cannot lose you."

Time stopped. Elizabeth's heart seized in her chest as she suddenly felt very foolish for

A Virtue of Marriage

antagonizing her cousin. Of course he would fear losing a loved one, she always forgot what little family he possessed.

"You shall not. You shall not lose me. I promise," she managed, as Darcy gripped her tighter.

Once satisfied, they shared a few kisses and Elizabeth extracted a resolution from Fitzwilliam that come tomorrow, he would help her with the Holbein family.

It wasn't until her door was again safely closed that Elizabeth crumpled to the bed, finally feeling the weight of her life on her slender shoulders. She could smell the lingering scent of Mr. Darcy's person in the room and exasperated, she grabbed a pillow from her left side and promptly deposited it across her face and groaned. She scolded herself that only heroines in novels suffered such dramatic love trials and at least her forbidden love was only postponed, not ruined forever.

Chapter Twenty-Four

The carriage stopped in front of Darcy House by mid-afternoon as for once in her life, Caroline Bingley did not tarry for a trip. She had planned her arrival with great cunning and waited in the foyer of one of the largest town homes on the row.

"Miss Bingley! How long it has been since we have seen you!" George Wickham stumbled out in the hallway from the direction of the kitchen corridor, holding a glass in his hand.

Caroline sniffed and held her chin high. She was no stranger to the abhorrent flirtations of George Wickham and observed him shunned by the other men enough times to know where her loyalties must lie.

"I'm here to see Georgiana. I've just returned to town."

"Ppppssshsh, Georgie is probably upstairs. Crying. In her room." He haphazardly leaned against the banister as he nearly tumbled to look up above him at the movement coming down. "That's all she finds time for these days."

Georgiana Wickham appeared at the top of the stairs, descending with a slump to her shoulders and red rims around her trademark blue eyes. "Miss Bingley, I am pleased to see you," she said, with little life to her voice.

Caroline gave a fake gasp and started up the stairs to meet Georgiana part of the way. "My goodness, you look unwell. Had I known you were doing this poorly... well, I'd have come straight away!"

Georgiana perked up at the first ray of friendship she had enjoyed since her marriage. "You mean, you only just arrived in London?" She allowed herself to be guided up the stairs by the older woman.

"Of course! I arrived this week with my brother Charles and dear sister Jane, and I planned to call tomorrow. You sounded so sad in your letter, I just knew in my heart something was wrong. I had to see that you were fine, and clearly, you are not my dear!"

They arrived at Georgiana's bedroom as her maid opened the door for the two women. As Caroline helped her friend to her bed, the young bride looked up at her desperately. "I know it's last minute, and horribly presumptuous on my part, but could you stay here at Darcy House? It would mean the world to me."

Caroline Bingley tried not to smile like a cat just capturing a canary and instead looked down as she patted Georgiana's arm. "If it's what you want, just say the word and I will stay."

This confused Georgiana who wondered if she had made another faux pas, and she began tearing up. "I thought—I mean, I just tried to."

Caroline laughed hollowly, trying to change her tone to that of a friendly giggle and not a mean laugh at Georgiana's lack of social prowess. "Certainly, I will go now and send for my things to be placed in a guest chamber and see about a tray being made up for you? Hmmm? And then you and I can sit and talk all about what's happened in London while I was banished to some God-forsaken country estate."

Before Caroline could leave, Georgiana pushed herself up to speak more loudly. "Was it really all bad?"

"Truly Georgiana, wait until I tell you about a woman with four daughters to marry off and how she chases every eligible man with her praises for him and her daughters, while waving a handkerchief and complaining about her nerves! And one of the daughters was sent away I hear, for such lewd behavior, even her cousin would not marry her!" Caroline pantomimed a brief impersonation of Mrs. Bennet before exiting the room.

For just a brief moment, a slight smile played on Georgiana's lips before she collapsed back against the familiar shape of her pillows. Her nightmares since attending that diner party with her husband would not abate and Georgiana needed the comfort of a friend. Those men had used her so meanly, just thinking of their hands touching her person, her husband watching with a gleam in his eye, Georgiana began to tremble and sob. She could never tell a soul what she did for George. And with Caroline Bingley present, perhaps she would never have to do such debased actions again. Her husband managed to accrue the monies he needed, and though George promised her a life she deserved, she wasn't sure she would survive a life as the wife of George Wickham.

Chapter Twenty-Five

Pandemonium broke out at Hunsford Cottage when word of Lady Catherine de Bourgh's imminent arrival reached the ears of William Collins. Shouting orders at the staff, his wife, and most importantly his wayward cousin Elizabeth Bennet, the sitting room became a flurry of activity just as the wheels of the phaeton rolled to a stop on the main drive just outside the home.

Elizabeth could not resist rushing to the window to peek out at the grand Dames condescension to visit the lowly parsonage. Her eyes recognized the smiling round face of Mr. Darcy's regular driver, Peter Holbein. She had met the man just that morning when he accompanied her and Fitzwilliam on their visit to the impoverished Holbein family living on the glebe lands her cousin managed. Catching his eye, the driver slowly nodded and slid one finger to the side of his nose.

Before she could work out a plan to go outside, Mr. Collins was seating Lady Catherine in the sitting room. Elizabeth frowned and took a seat on the far sofa as the Collinses fussed and fretted over the grand lady just as she was accustomed. On this visit, Lady Catherine waved her arms as if to swat a fly and shoo her parson and his wife away from her.

"There can be no mistake as to why I have deigned to travel here personally and explain why despite the Archbishop of Canterbury's arrival to Rosings this very afternoon, none in this household are invited to dine with us this evening. And the fault lies with no other than this hussy you continue to shelter in your home."

"Lady Catherine, we are most humble to receive your ladyship on any such occasion. And any offense my cousin has given, I most heartily apologize and beg your forgiveness." Mr. Collins bowed so low before her ladyship that he was very nearly prostrate.

"It is her very existence that offends!"

Elizabeth Bennet could not help herself and smiled at the imposing lady, infuriating her more.

"There! There –" Lady Catherine pointed a long fat finger directly at Elizabeth, "see how she laughs at us? She is guilty I say, guilty of attempting to bewitch my nephews with her arts and allurements. Women of her ilk have a road in London and should not be socializing with families of good standing."

"Your ladyship is mistaken, perhaps what might be the first time of any such occurrence. I am merely an acquaintance of your nephews, one of them only because he nearly killed me with his horse." Elizabeth slowly exhaled to restore her decorum.

"I was present in the same county and social gatherings with your nephew Mr. Darcy and my friend, and never was there any sign of impropriety or affection on either party." Charlotte Collins said quietly.

"Do not speak unless spoken to, Mrs. Collins," Mr. Collins hissed at his wife in a hoarse whisper.

"But –" Charlotte began to defend your friend, but elected to stop when her husband glared at her.

"Regardless of your own estimation of your behavior, as your moral and social superior, I say otherwise. Women of your profession are not suitable for His Grace's presence. Your utter lack of deference for your betters has barred you from this evening's festivities and any future visits of Rosings. This is my final word on the subject." Lady Catherine rose and nodded pertly at her parson. Unfortunately, the target of her vitriol was far from conceding the match.

Gazing determinedly out the window, Elizabeth spoke: "I wonder how much weight your word shall have once you are the dowager of Rosings and no longer the mistress?"

Lady Catherine turned around slowly with her face ever increasing in shades of red. "You would dare to insult a peer?"

"No your ladyship, I only humbly make the observation your nephew, Mr. Darcy, is set to wed your daughter now the Archbishop has arrived. My cousin has most emphatically championed the blessed event my entire visit. Once that occurs, it will be for Mr. and Mrs. Darcy to determine who shall and shall not visit Rosings."

"Cousin Elizabeth, I believe you should retire to your room and pack your belongings." Mr. Collins said through clenched teeth.

"I expressly forbid it!" Lady Catherine called out. Peering at the young upstart, the older woman took great joy in issuing yet another edict. "I desire this trumped up bit of muslin remain in your home until after the wedding. Then she may cry herself all the way back to London and whatever relations will take her in. Once my daughter marries, my nephew will soon tire of your company, mark my words. Men never stay true to their mistresses, because as you get older, their tastes stay young."

"Then lucky for me I am not the mistress of either of your nephews. And I find it a slander for you to continue to blacken my character, your ladyship." Elizabeth Bennet rose from the couch and pursed her lips. She knew she ought to behave better, but this woman who had everything yet made all around her miserable tried every ounce of her dwindling patience. Momentarily closing her eyes, Elizabeth thought of her Fitzwilliam, remembering that after tomorrow, he would be free.

"What's that she's doing? Closing her eyes like that, open them I say! Don't trifle with me young lady and then pretend to swoon. I won't have it!"

Elizabeth sighed and lowered herself into a deep curtsy. Before rising, she made her apologies. "Forgive me, my tongue has ran away with me. I am, as you say, unfit for civilized company. With your permission, Cousin Collins, I shall retire to my room and reflect on what my behavior has cost you in my friend."

"Yes, yes, I do believe that is best. Come, come, you have vexed her ladyship too much.

Forgive us, Lady Catherine, for this evening's continued offenses."

Elizabeth scurried around her ladyship and passed her cousin to take the stairs as quickly as a lady might. Hopefully, she had done just enough damage to keep Lady Catherine from suspecting the true plans tomorrow, and permitted to retire early, she was certain to rise with the sun in time for the ceremony. Pulling out bread and a small bottle of wine her maid Anna had smuggled from the kitchens the first time Mr. Collins withheld food from her, Elizabeth found her appetite fleeting with the excitement of a wedding on the horizon.

Chapter Twenty-Six

Longbourn grew dramatically in size in the perceptions of Catherine Bennet as yet another sister was off on a grand adventure, yet she remained home. Just that afternoon, Lydia Bennet, the youngest Bennet sister, was invited as the distinguished guest of Mrs. Foster, the Colonel's wife, to follow the militia to Brighton for the spring and summer drills. Kitty Bennet tried to not take her ire out on the poor watercolor she was making of a vase with wilted flowers when her peace and quiet were disturbed by the only remaining Bennet sister still at home, her older sister Mary.

A Virtue of Marriage

"You know Mama shall be cross to see your paint set again. Why must you antagonize her so?"

The paint set was another gift from the Bennet sister who must not be mentioned, Elizabeth, and arrived as an early Easter gift to the post. Kitty now had half a dozen art pieces for her sister that she planned to bind in a portfolio with her next month's pin money. She didn't dare send her sister anything in return, but still held out hope that one day, the family might heal. Her sentiments directly echoed those of her Aunt Gardiner's.

"You're doing it wrong. Look at how big your vase is compared to your table. It's too big." Mary criticized, looking over Kitty's shoulder.

The statement was too much as Kitty looked down and saw that her sister was right. In a fit, Catherine Bennet seized her artwork and crumpled it to a small ball and threw it at her sister who was now backing away slowly.

"There, are you happy? You harpy! Why, why can you never mind your own business?"

"Don't take your frustrations out on me. It is not my fault Lydia was allowed to go to Brighton and you were not invited."

"It's not fair! Lizzie is away in London. You got to go to Bath. When will it be MY turn?" Kitty slammed her paint set closed with a flip of her fingers and swished her brush most vigorously to remove all color.

Mary shrugged and lay on the extra bed now in Kitty's room. "You mustn't speak her name. Father has said we must not, and we must not."

"But why? What reasoning has ever been given? No one would have married that toad!"

"I would have. I would have married Mr. Collins, and you should not call him a toad!"

"Oh, you loved him did you? All his sermonizing and superior airs. Yes, I'm sure you would have made the happy couple until you found out what poor Charlotte had to the hard way."

Mary's ears perked up at the hint of gossip surrounding her beloved William. "What did Charlotte Lucas learn? Any fault of Mr. Collins is surely caused by an unsupportive wife."

"Wouldn't you like to know?"

"Tell me! It is a vicious lie, whatever it is."

Kitty shook her head. "No it's not, I heard it straight from Maria Lucas when she returned from Kent!"

"Tell me!"

Kitty mimed locking her lips, which only infuriated Mary more. Frantically looking around the room, Mary spied a favored bonnet by her sister and snagged it, threatening to rip it to shreds.

"No! You're no better than Lydia!"

"Where do you think she learned it?"

"Girls!" Mrs. Bennet shrill voice carried up the stairs and both Mary and Kitty realized their spat had gone too far. Kitty marched over to Mary and giving her a surprising shove, snatched the bonnet from her hands as she fell back towards the bed. Only Mary's feet slipped from underneath her and she landed on the hard wooden floor with a thud.

Kitty's eyes widened in fear as loud steps could be heard thundering up the stairs. A very angry Mrs. Bennet stood in the doorway as Mary began to sob and pointed her finger at Kitty.

"What is this? What have you done to poor Mary?"

"Nothing, Mama. She was going to rip my bonnet!" Kitty held up the bonnet as proof of her sister's treachery.

"She's painting again, and she won't stop talking about Lizzie," Mary whined as she continued to whimper from the floor.

"That's not true, tis not! I wouldn't tell her what Maria Lucas told me about Mr. Collins blackening Charlotte's eye during their visit, and she —"

"Enough!" Mrs. Bennet stormed past Kitty and collected the offending paint set as it sat next to the window.

"No, please! I so enjoy the painting, and it is an accomplishment!" Kitty pleaded.

"You wish to work on your accomplishments? Stitch. Read. No husband will want you with paint beneath your finger nails and your wild visions on paper!"

"Please, Mama!" But it was to no avail, Mrs. Bennet carried the paint set out of the room and Kitty sunk to the floor in sobs. After a few minutes, Mary ended her charade of being injured and slithered towards her sister forlorn before her.

"That's what you get for spreading lies!" Crawling backwards away from Kitty's reach, Mary rose and restored her dress and appearance before leaving the room herself.

Anger pounded and throbbed in Kitty's head until she screeched and clenched her fists at her side. Throwing herself upright, she rushed to the door and slammed it shut! A habit becoming too familiar in her life, Catherine Bennet, the surrogate for Elizabeth, cried herself to sleep.

Chapter Twenty-Seven

Lady Matlock reclined in her parlor nursing a most dreadful headache with her Cook's famous tea blend. A splash or two of brandy in the cup made the warm beverage a balm to sooth the Countess of Matlock's throbbing veins. Before her lay a complicated arrangement of invitations as the height of the London Season came into full swing. Many families would arrive from the country as Easter was the following weekend, but given the scandals of Georgiana and now Fitzwilliam and the girl from the theatre, the Matlocks had elected to remain in town to help parry whispers.

Sipping a long draft from her fine china, the sound of a carriage rolling up to the house outside piqued her interest. While dressed impeccably for the day and able to accept callers, truly Margaret Fitzwilliam had no interest in playing social games as she still suffered from late hours of the previous evening's ball at Lady Sefton's town home.

Relief washed over her as her dear husband strolled into the parlor, until she viewed his expression.

"Reginald, sit down. You look as if you are to suffer an apoplexy." His wife beckoned for him to find a chair. Instead, the Earl of Matlock paced the parlor floor in front of the grand windows looking out upon the busy street.

"That son of yours, Margaret, shall be the death of us."

"Which son is that pray tell? We do have two."

"Richard! I had business with our solicitor and I notice papers with his name written upon them. Now, I ask you, what business does Richard have with our lawyers that I am not aware of? I know he confides in you."

Margaret Fitzwilliam mulled for a moment, and continued sipping her tea.

The Earl halted in his track as this wife's playacting and stormed over to her table in a deliberate double-quick march. Placing both hands on the edge, he peered closely until his nose was directly in front of his wife's teacup that she held so delicately. "Margaret, tell me what you know."

Lady Matlock leaned back in her chair and fluttered away her husband's face with a slight wave of her hand. Reginald returned to a standing position and folded his arms across his chest. The position was a similar stance he shared with both of his sons, a similarity Margaret always found highly amusing.

"I have not spoken to Richard in weeks. Why not visit him at his barracks and seek your answers directly from him?"

"I did just as you say and he's not there! He's gone! I was told by some bloke in a red coat the Colonel has leave and is visiting his relations in Kent!'"

Lady Matlock gasped.

"Margaret, I'm going to ask you this once more. What is our son planning and where is he?"

"He wouldn't . . . they wouldn't . . ." Margaret Fitzwilliam's furrowed her brows and placed her teacup down. She flattened her palms against her temples and pushed as she tried to find any evidence her supposition was wrong. Surely those two boys did not think they could take on their Aunt Catherine, alone, without reinforcements?

"We must ready the carriage. We must leave for Rosings at once!"

"Whatever for?" The Earl of Matlock called after his wife as she hastily stood up from the table and began pulling on cords to summon the housekeeper. There was much to plan and little time to accomplish it all.

"Richard's going to marry Anne, and your negotiations with the Duke of Northumberland will fall to shambles."

"What!" The Earl roared, much in a similar fashion as his son. The Earl's lip glistened with perspiration and his wife approached him to place her hand on his arms.

"I'm certain we shall be there in time. If Darcy and Richard had pulled off this coup, we both know Catherine would be standing and shouting in our parlor at this very moment."

Still the Earl said nothing and only breathed huskily in and out. Finally, he listened to his wife's good sense.

"We shall leave tomorrow, I cannot miss the dinner tonight at the Burrells. If they have not accomplished it as yet, tis better I shore up any loose ends now."

Chapter Twenty-Eight

Chirping birds harkened the arrival of dawn as Elizabeth Bennet shivered in the morning's crisp start. Taking a moment to collect a few blooms along the way, she worried not that the bottom of her best gown showed several inches of the grass's dew. Her breath caught in her chest, as standing outside the small chapel on the north side of the estate was her Fitzwilliam, dressed impeccably in a suit of the finest cut in a pale gray.

"Good morning, sir, it looks to be a glorious day for a wedding!" She called out as she turned onto the front of the chapel's outdoor path. Walking down a perfect aisle from the shrubbery around her, with the blossoms for Anne firmly in her hand, Fitzwilliam Darcy turned to see a

A Virtue of Marriage

vision of his loveliest dream walking towards him with the sun's glory illuminating around her.

As Elizabeth approached, he extended his hand to accept hers and bowed over it to kiss the top, careful to nip just above her petite glove.

"Good morning, madam, I am only sorry to say the wedding should be for another couple."

Elizabeth smiled and cocked her head to one side. With a heavy sigh, she felt surprised to feel tears prick the edges of her eyes. She shook her head, determined not to cry before the ceremony even began, and sniffed. "Our time is near, Fitzwilliam. I am afraid once we return to Hertfordshire, my father might insist upon a proper courtship." Elizabeth giggled and took a step back so that Mr. Darcy could open the chapel door.

Inside the stone abbey was aglow with candles, and Miss de Bourgh's long time companion Mrs. Annesley and her maid, Harriet, sat in the small pews. The bride was prettily seated in an ornate chair provided for her health and Elizabeth happily took her place as witness. As the men discussed the license and particulars with the exalted Archbishop of Canterbury, Elizabeth suddenly felt very shy to see Fitzwilliam's godfather.

"Are those for me?" Anne inquired, noticing Elizabeth looking uncomfortable.

Elizabeth nodded and handed her wildflower bouquet to her friend and hopefully one day, cousin.

"They are so beautiful. You should not have troubled."

"I understand that if there is ever a day to undertake any troubles for any one, it is most certainly for a bride on her wedding day!" Elizabeth laughed and noticed Mrs. Annesley nodded sagely while Harriet covered her giggle.

"If we may proceed, the grace of our Lord Jesus Christ, the love of our God, and the fellowship of the Holy Spirit be with you." His Grace began the service.

"And also with you," those in attendance responded.

The marriage ceremony was identical to the ceremony Elizabeth watched for Jane and Mr. Bingley, only this time her gaze could not leave the face of the male witness. As Richard and Anne took their vows to love, cherish, and protect one another, Elizabeth and Fitzwilliam could only stand silently, each wishing to make the same declarations.

The service ended with communion for all and as Elizabeth knelt for a blessing from the Archbishop, she was stunned when the older man looked at her with kind eyes and proclaimed:

"You will do well for my Fitzwilliam. Blessed be your life, Elizabeth Bennet."

She nodded, not knowing what to say, the solemnity of the moment weighing too heavily on her conscience. Briefly, doubts of being strong enough to become his wife flashed across her mind, but she closed her eyes and relished in the peace of love. If the Archbishop of Canterbury was certain, who was a young miss from Hertfordshire to contradict him?

The smile did not stay away long from Lizzie's lips and it was all much too soon that Fitzwilliam was walking her back towards the parsonage as the sun was now high enough to be early morning. Arm in arm, as it no longer mattered who saw them together, for Anne and Richard were bound in Holy Matrimony, Elizabeth felt herself slow her pace as it suddenly felt wrong to leave Fitzwilliam's side.

"I have spoken to Father Charles and he is most intrigued by your cousin's management of the parish."

"But a living cannot be revoked except for extreme misconduct . . ."

Darcy nodded as they reached the path where they must break away unless he was to walk her to the parsonage. Both of them stopped.

"Can you bear four more days, Fitzwilliam?" Elizabeth asked earnestly, biting her lower lip.

"Four days? Whatever for, Elizabeth? I am free! Free to whisk you away this very minute to seek your father's permission and to Gretna Green if need be!"

As he twirled them about in a rare bubbling over of his emotions, Elizabeth laughed. The meadow around her became a blur of colors. When they stopped, she regained her focus from the momentary dizziness.

"I fear for Charlotte. And I have not visited yet a fortnight, after we leave, I do not know when we shall return, do you?"

Darcy frowned, and quickly recovered remembering how intently his beloved Elizabeth studied his face. "I cannot play the offended suitor. Richard asked me to stay on for a few days at most to see to a smooth transition of the estate. He may need to ride to London himself should our Aunt fight their wedding."

"Fight it? Surely she cannot seek an annulment when The Most Reverend presided . . . I mean, who on earth would challenge such a wedding?"

Darcy wiped his chin with his hand, imagining the sheer preposterous situation his Lizzie just evoked. "You do not know my Aunt,

I would not be surprised if she sought Prinny's help. The man's opinion can almost always be purchased."

A crow crying off in the distance distracted the happy couple back to their present aims. Darcy's hand delicately traced Elizabeth's jaw and very softly he kissed her lips.

"Fitzwilliam . . ."

"No my darling, today should have been a double wedding. This madness has gone on long enough. May the world know Fitzwilliam Darcy, Master of Pemberley, Carver, and Darcy House in London is caught, and he prays his future wife shall never let him go."

The pretty speech made Elizabeth blush and she looked up at him through her eyelashes. With a heavy sigh, she released her grip on his arms and walked a few steps backwards.

"You ought to go back, soon as Lady Catherine finds out about the wedding, Richard and Anne will need you."

Darcy nodded and bowed sweepingly low for his intended bride out of respect. The mantle he was asking this young woman to wear would not be light, but he had no doubt the caliber of her character would more than carry her through this trying time and all future ones.

This time, it was Fitzwilliam who watched Elizabeth's lithe figure walk forlornly towards the cottage her cousin lived in. Once she rounded the bend in the road, Darcy adjusted his hat and turned on his heel to head the hundred yards towards Rosings. He would not miss his Aunt's apprising of her dowager status for the world.

Chapter Twenty-Nine

Elation over the wedding ceremony and her future by Mr. Darcy's side evaporated as soon as Elizabeth carefully closed the side kitchen door to the parsonage.

"There you are, Cousin Elizabeth. I was getting a little nervous."

His voice chilled Elizabeth to the bone and the small hairs on the back of her neck stood up. Hunched over the door handle, she slowly craned her face around her shoulder to see her cousin, Mr. Collins sitting calmly at the worktable. For a brief moment, neither of them moved, as soon as Elizabeth began to turn he grabbed and dragged her from the kitchen by the forearm.

Elizabeth cried out in pain as his grip and twist was thrice the strength he had employed before.

"Nasty, conniving, trollop that does not deserve a shred of dignity . . ." he muttered on and on as many insulting epithets as he managed with Elizabeth struggling against his aims. With a harsh toss, he cast Elizabeth to the floor; she barely braced her fall, further injuring her twisted arm.

"Stop! Mr. Collins, perhaps she has an explanation. Lizzie, you have an explanation, tell my husband why you are dressed . . . and out . . ." Charlotte Collins looked at her friend upon the floor from the safety of the stairs, as if the bannister and railing provided some magical barrier to Mr. Collins' anger. As Charlotte's eyes widened at the damning evidence before her, Elizabeth raised her arms defensively looking towards her friend.

The first slap stung Elizabeth's cheek before she had any warning and her face turned most violently in the direction of the force.

"Look at her! Who did you rendezvous with? Out with it! Which man made you his whore that you sneak out at the break of dawn to meet your liaisons?" Collins reached forward to lift up Elizabeth's dress as if looking for proof of her dalliances. Elizabeth smacked his hands away as she screamed again, pulling her gown down and scurrying backwards as much as she could manage.

"You are mad! Absolutely mad! I've not had any such liaisons!"

"Lizzie, do not lie. He hates it when you lie," Charlotte advised, again distracting Elizabeth briefly before another slap met her face.

Truly angry, Elizabeth scrambled to stand and picked up the closest object she could find. The book flew wide, not coming even close to Mr. Collins' person. She continued to back away from his menacing presence.

"I am not lying! I went for a walk, which I know, is against the rules, but I had to get out. I had to walk in God's great cathedral of nature."

"Do not dare speak of our Heavenly Father, your words are a displeasure to Him. You defy every person of authority and expect no retribution. Oh, retribution is coming." Collins reached behind him to pull a crop from the side table. Raising it high, he brought it down with such force, Elizabeth only barely managed to shield her face, though her arm felt on fire from the blow.

"I witnessed your treachery, kissing an engaged man out in the open!" Another blow came down, but Elizabeth managed to dodge just at the last moment causing Mr. Collins to stumble forward and grasp the mantle to steady himself.

"I kissed my fiancée! Mr. Darcy is to marry me!"

" Lies!" Collins roared turning and rushing towards Elizabeth who tipped the armchair at the last possible second to thwart him once more.

Ducking below the legs of the upturned chair, Elizabeth cowered and prepared to lift up on the chair again in defense.

"Anne and Richard married this morning. Mr. Darcy and I stood witness as His Grace performed the ceremony." Elizabeth flinched as she breathed easier, expecting his temper to calm once he heard the truth.

As she opened her eyes, a moment passed. The last thing Elizabeth Bennet saw was Charlotte's mouth open wide in a scream.

Chapter Thirty

Hours later, Elizabeth woke with a vile taste in her mouth and instinctively leaned over as she began to toss up the liquid contents of her stomach onto the bare floor. Her head spun so mercilessly, the creak of the bedroom door took a moment to register in her throbbing head. Once it did, she cried in panic and rolled off the bed to retreat to the far side of the room, an action that immediately flooded her senses with pain once she stopped.

"Miss, miss . . . " Anna, the maid who traveled with Elizabeth whispered just inside the door jamb. "Come quickly, there's not much time."

"Where . . ." Elizabeth's voice broke in a sob she managed to silence with a gulp of air, "where is he?"

"He sleeps. Hurry, there's no time." Anna's hand beckoned her employer's niece to leave as she stood lookout.

Elizabeth tried to stand, but found she could not properly manage. Half crawling, half stumbling, she made it to the door only to find the room and stairs spinning madly out of focus. She blinked and blinked, and could see that Mrs. Plummer, the kind cook, stood by ready to open the front door. Despite the pain and nausea, Elizabeth managed to remember how she traversed the stairs back when her ankle was broken.

Although unladylike, she scooted and slid step by step, holding onto the railing to steady herself though her eyes told her she was as if adrift in the ocean. As she reached the front door, Mrs. Plummer hastily opened it and the noise startled Mr. Collins napping in his study.

As Elizabeth heard his voice call out, adrenaline took over and she bolted out the door, vaguely hearing it slam behind her. For a moment she thought to run to Rosings, but feared Collins would catch up with her assuming she'd go in that direction. Turning around, she ran south.

She fell and got back up what must have been a dozen times. Her hands shook in pain, caked in mud, but she refused to stop. What felt like an eternity brought her to the doorstep of a familiar place and slumped to the ground, she hit the door with all of the strength she had left.

The patting on the door barely registered a sound, and Elizabeth had no voice to call out with. Breathing labored, she kept banging on the door, or so she thought, until her strength and injuries threatened to overwhelm her.

"See Momma, Miss Bennet is here!" a young girl's voice cried out as she opened the door and Elizabeth spilled onto the floor of the Holbein cottage.

"Good Heavens! Petey, run now, fetch Mr. Darcy! Don't stop running, boy, all the way to the big house!" Diana Holbein shouted as she struggled forward though her advancing condition prevented her from moving easily. "Miss Bennet? Miss Bennet? You must wake dear and help me get you to a chair. Come, come, up we go now."

Elizabeth heard Diana Holbein's voice coming to her as if in a dream. Her mouth tasted funny again, and as she moved to retch, somehow she managed to lift herself with Diana's assistance. She apologized for the insult, but her words came out funny.

"Lord help me in heaven, whoever did this to you deserves a month in stocks!"

"Collins," Elizabeth spat out his name and she lolled her head, her neck not strong enough to hold her up.

"No, no, now you stay awake. Mr. Darcy will be here soon."

Elizabeth tried to look at Diana's face but she kept seeing two of the very nice woman. And she was so very tired. Why couldn't she just sleep until Fitzwilliam arrived?

"Elizabeth! Wake up!" Diana called out, keeping her vigil over the young woman. Her husband's career of a lumber jack had long taught her the danger of letting one sleep after a blow to the head. The men would poke and prod to keep a fellow jack alert as long as possible, twas the only chance for survival.

"Dear, you sleep now you may never wake up. It's a right nasty blow to your head from the bump on your brow." Mrs. Holbein accepted a small pail of cool water carried in with mighty effort by young Mary Jane. Dipping her apron into the water, she dabbed Elizabeth's face and the cold made her jerk in response.

"Ssh, careful, careful now love. Easy does it."

The sound of a horse outside the cottage announced the arrival of Mr. Darcy who stormed in without invitation. Spying his Elizabeth in a heap in the chair, he collapsed to the floor and took her into his arms just as Mrs. Holbein moved out of the way.

"Lizzie, my Lizzie. My darling, I'm here. I'm here."

"Fitz . . ." Elizabeth managed before slipping back out of consciousness.

Chapter Thirty-One

All remnants of sunlight were gone when Elizabeth next awoke. Before she could make the decision to move, a firm hand touched her arm.

"Please do not move. My physician is on his way from London but Simmons says you likely suffered another concussion. They are ..." Darcy swallowed and struggled to speak. His man came forward and bowed his head to the young woman, for even he had come to admire for her fortitude.

"Each blow to the head is harder on the mind, my lady." Simmons bowed his head again and stepped back, afraid he had overstepped his bounds. But he truly wished for this young woman to prevail; he had seen his master's massive fall from grace when he last thought he had lost her. Simmons had no desire to return to those dark days.

"Thank you, Simmons. Please tell my cousin she has awoken and I shall be ready presently. Then come back, if you please, and allow no one in this room."

The servant bowed low and quietly left the room.

"I am so sorry, Fitzwilliam." Elizabeth managed her words and felt pleased at least now she could string together a cohesive sentence.

Darcy bit his knuckle as he stared down at her. Once he found his composure, he talked as softly as he could. "It is my fault for allowing you near that excuse for a man after the first time he struck you. But fear not, he shall not pass this night without paying dearly for his transgression."

Panic washed over Elizabeth as she began to fret and found frustration, as she could not again speak clearly. "No . . . no hurt . . . trouble for you."

Fitzwilliam's expression softened, as he understood the look in her eyes, the same beautiful eyes that made dizzying circuits as they struggled to steady their aim. A pair of fine eyes, indeed. She was so very injured and still her first instinct was to protect him.

Leaning down to gently kiss her injured face and forehead, Darcy deeply inhaled her scent.

"There will be justice tonight, Elizabeth. There will be justice, and the law shall not touch me."

"But —" she managed, before he placed a finger to her lips. Loud voices could be heard outside in the hall just as the door to her room burst open. The Colonel came in with an older couple close behind, all three squabbling.

"Think son! He is a parson! The headlines shall read 'Rogue Colonel Beats Clergy!'" the older man cried out.

"Richard, sleep on it. The parson is not going anywhere, you can easily . . ." the elegant woman's voice trailed off as she spied the sorry state of the woman in the bed. "Lations!"

The older man grasped the woman before she fainted, but she patted his support away.

Perplexed, Elizabeth's head began a new steady pounding in her ears as the blood felt too pinched inside. "I apologize if I look badly." Again, she cheered herself on making sense. Maybe she only needed practice to keep speaking correctly.

"There she is! Lord and Lady Matlock, please meet Miss Elizabeth Bennet, the strongest, funniest, most charismatic woman of my acquaintance and soon to be my cousin as soon as Darcy manages the paperwork. Miss Bennet, these are my parents."

Elizabeth tried to move her head, but Darcy's hand on her shoulder reminded her she was not to move. Instead, she blinked a number of times and tried to smile, but realized her lip felt swollen and would not move.

Lady Matlock glided around the bed and waited for her nephew Darcy to vacate his chair. He refused at first, but Richard gave a low whistle, and Darcy, with a pained look in his face, reluctantly complied.

"Aunt Maddie—"

"Simmons is here, Catherine will not come near, upon my word."

Darcy breathed a sigh of relief. Richard clasped him on the shoulders and the worried suitor shed his misery for the courage of a knight, charged with availing his Lady Love of her treacherous cousin.

Just as the men were about to leave, whispering quietly of their plans, Lady Matlock grasped Elizabeth's hand and looked again on the poor woman's battered face.

"Boys, take Declan with you."

"Mother?" Richard paused to make sure he understood his mother's order.

The Countess of Matlock turned away from one of the worst crimes she had personally seen perpetrated and glared at her son with the fire of true Fitzwilliam.

"And if you do not kill the man, leave Declan there in the service of Mrs. Collins."

Chapter Thirty-Two

Caroline Bingley rose earlier than she was inclined, a woman on a mission and no time to fail. If her calculations were correct from Eliza's last letter to her sister, Mr. Darcy would be leaving Kent at any moment after his cousin married the sickly de Bourgh girl. Then, he would be free to see Caroline for the dutiful spouse she was educated to be, and the first part of that plan involved learning why all of the furnishings and décor were mysteriously disappearing.

She had already plied that simpering Georgiana for details, but any mention of potential financial challenges and the girl began to cry buckets! Sentimentality was an asset in many a lady, but not possessed by the mercenary

Caroline Bingley. She had no time for such useless, futile emotions. Feelings warped one's perspective of their goals.

Aggravated to conduct her own toilette, the necessary denigration would keep her plan a secret. Being a guest at Darcy House for over a week she watched the Wickhams most carefully. They were never in the same room together, aside from the occasional meal. And twice now Caroline had tried to seek Georgiana's weaker state after retiring for the evening to find her suite of rooms locked. All was certainly not as it seemed, this was no love match.

Tiptoeing into the Master's study, Caroline froze when a loud snore startled her progress. She whipped her face towards the sofa along the far wall to spy a lounging George Wickham, splayed in half dress along the length. Cursing her bad luck, she moved gingerly, wondering why the man had not stayed out all night like all others, but decided there was no time like the present to settle one's destiny. Darcy might arrive any day, and without the truth, he would cast her aside as an afterthought like so many times before.

Carefully, Caroline shifted the papers on the desk, moving the ink pots and letter opener to the very edge of the desk. A missive about mines in Derby, signed with the seal of Lord

Strange piqued her interest immediately. The wedding of Thomas Stanley to that milquetoast Sarah Milbanke was the event of the season, the wedding of the year! But the Viscount was hardly in control of such sums of money, something was amiss.

Scrambling to find more information, Caroline forgot her need to be quiet and it was only when she realized the snoring had stopped that a pit in her stomach dropped to somewhere around her knees. Looking up from her shady endeavors she found herself staring directly into the blue eyes of none other than George Wickham.

"Miss Bingley, I had no idea you had such a head for business." George Wickham's normal debonair style fell flat as a sobering belch interrupted his sentiments.

Repulsed, Caroline wrinkled her nose and waved the offending airs away. "As a longtime friend of the Darcy family, I felt strongly that my interest for Mr. Darcy and Georgiana were paramount in looking into these affairs. You've pared down this home a great deal and I'm curious as to what you expect to happen to replace your theft before Mr. Darcy returns?"

George Wickham's jawline tensed and a lesser woman would have cowered. Not Caroline. The half-drunk man stumbled around the desk to come closer to her person, and Caroline watched as he used the edge to steady himself ever so often with mild amusement.

"It is very dangerous to come along and accuse a man such of myself of criminal activity. I believe you have miscalculated Miss Bingley in the extent of my gentility."

His hand reached out for the woman, his mind anxious for violence, his body's coordination less capable. In a thrice, Caroline snatched the letter opener in front of her and slashed his hand, just above the wrist, making him cry out and recoil.

"You cut me! How dare you!"

Caroline pursed her lips and gave a swift push on the already teetering man so he fell backwards, knocking his head most satisfying on the globe behind him. Dazed and laying contentedly on the floor, Caroline collected the most damning pieces of parchment before looking one last time over the listless body of George Wickham. The drink would wear off, no doubt, but for a time, he was harmless.

"Please, I've parried more vicious attacks in a ballroom," she scoffed, taking great pleasure to plant a determined stomp at the crux of his legs. His cries and moans bothered her none as she left the study, satisfied she exacted some revenge for the miserable baggage sobbing herself to sleep each night above stairs.

Chapter Thirty-Three

Mid-morning at Rosings was a somber affair. Elizabeth's sick room became a regular stop as people came in and left to check on her. Such attentions frightened Elizabeth as Fitzwilliam could not be present the whole time, and she had in fact not seen him since last night. Worry, fatigue, and her vulnerable position made her convalescence an absolute torture.

Mr. Darcy's personal physician, Doctor Matthews, did his best to inquire discretely about all of her injuries, but with Lady Matlock in the room, Elizabeth's mortification over the entire ordeal won out.

A Virtue of Marriage

"I'm terribly sorry, Miss Bennet, but I must ask. Did your cousin violate any personal privacy?"

"No, nothing of the kind. He was angry, he was not depraved." Elizabeth sat up further in the bed, adamant to will herself healthy again.

"Miss Bennet, please, I must advise for you to rest and lay down properly. Mr. Darcy will be very cross—"

"It's quite alright, Doctor. Mr. Darcy is well aware there is little I do properly and he has accustomed himself to my faults." Elizabeth wished to jump from the bed in joy that her mental faculties seemed fully returned. She checked for offense to Lady Matlock, Darcy's aunt that she had to say was a considerable improvement over the other relation of her acquaintance, but saw none. Instead the Colonel's mother appeared to enjoy her small jest.

The examination stopped when Mr. Darcy himself appeared, well dressed and attended to by his man. Elizabeth smiled and reached out to him, full of glee when he quickly came around to the other side of her sickbed. Grasping his hands, she immediately noticed his injuries.

"Fitzwilliam! You are hurt!"

Slightly sheepish, Darcy held out his hands and flexed them. Visible bruising and swelling bubbled around his knuckles, but he was certain none were broken.

"A most satisfying injury, my dear. Fear not."

"But you must be attended to, there Dr. Matthews, see to his hands please. I am perfectly fine and fit, just a slight set back." Elizabeth made sure not to wince as she settled the blankets more properly around her person. Her effects and Anna had arrived early this morning and she was very grateful to the maid in helping her change out of her ruined gown covered in blood, mud, and grass stains.

"How is she? This is her second head injury as I told you."

Elizabeth frowned as her Fitzwilliam spoke about her like she was not there. Doctor Matthews replied that while the short-term effects were promising, it was still too early to say she was without permanent injury.

"Oh for pity's sakes! Lady Matlock, might I have a word in private with your nephew?" Elizabeth looked to the matron for support. She hoped she measured the woman correctly and felt relieved when her ally agreed, provided she might send Anna in. Elizabeth agreed and poor Doctor Matthews found himself swept out of the room and Fitzwilliam stunned at the sheer efficiency in which women work.

A Virtue of Marriage

Gently, Elizabeth patted her bed to motion for Darcy to sit on the edge, a scandalous proposition, but she had a feeling they were far beyond the bounds of propriety in the strictures of the relationship. Fitzwilliam complied, if for no other reason to become closer to his Elizabeth for his and her own comfort.

"Fitzwilliam, I wish to leave this place."

"Certainly, in a week or two, when you are recovered—"

"No, sir, I wish to leave within the hour, this very moment it may be managed. I am not safe here, I have visions of Lady Catherine barging in at any moment."

"She is heavily sedated, a recommendation of Dr. Smeads I can finally agree with."

Elizabeth turned slightly, sucking in her breath at the pain in her rib cage. Exhaling, she looked her Fitzwilliam in the eye and did not break contact.

"We must leave. To London. I cannot explain, but I know in my heart this place is too precarious. Lady Catherine cannot be kept unconscious forever. The Colonel and Anne have his parents to support them, we must leave."

Taking another deep breath, she begged. "Rescue me, Fitzwilliam, take me away from this awful, awful place."

Elizabeth sobbed as she collapsed forward into Darcy's chest, crying until she felt no more tears could possibly fall. The evil memories invoked by the doctor's examination overwhelmed her and she wished with all of her might to erase the horrors of the parsonage's sitting room.

Deep in Darcy's own soul a damn broke of the emotion he had held back. He had made a mistake once in not protecting her, he would not make another.

"As you wish, madame. As you wish."

Chapter Thirty-Four

The Darcy carriage was packed and readied for travel as swiftly as the staff could manage. The equipage took no pause at the parsonage for a farewell, Elizabeth too upset at her friend's complicit actions during her attack. Sitting on a bench in Mr. Darcy's arms with her maid Anna across from her, the nausea and throbbing headache returned almost immediately.

Refusing to say she was too unwell to travel, Elizabeth Bennet willed herself to sleep to keep from vomiting in Mr. Darcy's fine carriage. Her mind fractured in its thoughts, she tried to think of happier times and could not seem to pull from the well of her memories. The panic of feeling trapped in the hell of her mind made her tense, and Mr. Darcy soothed her with calming words.

Each bump and rut pained her bruised body, her porcelain skin marred in too many places just under her dress. The hours to London were long until on the last portion of the trip, Elizabeth finally managed to sleep. It was a change in the road's texture that woke her, embarrassingly lying fully in Mr. Darcy's lap.

She tried to move too quickly, and cried out in pain. Darcy hastened to assist her, lest she further injure herself.

"Forgive me, Elizabeth, I did not mean to allow you fall into such a position, but you were finally sleeping, I had not the heart to move you."

Regaining her bearings, Elizabeth looked out the window only to regret that action immediately. Even at the carriages slow pace through the crowded streets of London, the world outside moved too fast for her eyes to handle.

"Should we stop at Gracechurch Street? I am certain your aunt and uncle would listen to our explanations." Darcy waited to hear Elizabeth's wishes, unwilling to say what a disastrous idea he thought those plans to be, but neither did he wish to prey upon her vulnerable state.

Elizabeth looked at Anna, the poor maid assigned to her by those same relations. A small shrug provided little reassurances for Elizabeth, but she made her decision.

"No, I believe it best we go to your home, Mr. Darcy. The scandal of Kent will not remain in that county long, and my appearance is too ghastly for calm interpretations."

"You are perfectly lovely—"

"Mr. Darcy, I did gaze into a hand glass this morning. Save your breath for your stew, sir."

Comforted by her humor and wit, Darcy squeezed his beloved's hand in response.

"Will your staff find me so horrifically wanton?"

"Are you mad, woman? I mean you've suffered a blow to the head, but Mrs. Potter is wrapped around your smallest finger in all of the best ways. My staff will be honored to aid the illustrious Elizabeth Bennet in her recovery." Darcy's breath tickled Elizabeth's neck as he huskily explained her position as far as he was concerned just as the carriage rolled to a stop in front of his town home.

With Darcy and Anna's aid, Elizabeth managed to walk down the path to bright red door of Number 12, Grosvenor Square. The door opened by a footman allowed a cacophony of yells and shrieks to billow out of the house.

"What's this?" Darcy asked, an angry edge to his voice.

Inside the entrance hall, the Wickhams were arguing loudly with Caroline Bingley perched high up on the stairs adding her own two bits to the fray. Footmen, maids, and other staff stood sentry along the edges of the entranceway, leery, but to frightened to go near the snarling, crazed George Wickham.

All parties of the disagreement ceased upon the spectacle of Mr. Darcy's sudden appearance with what appeared to be a half-dead woman on his arm.

"What is she doing here?" Caroline sneered from above, shattering the silence.

"I might ask the same of you, Miss Bingley!" Darcy boomed, feeling guilty as Elizabeth flinched beside him. "Mrs. Potter?" Darcy looked around the room until the housekeeper pushed forward. "Please see Miss Bennet and her maid to a guest suite. Give them every accommodation, Doctor Matthews shall visit this evening."

"Certainly, sir, come you poor dear." The matronly arms of Mrs. Potter were just the comfort Elizabeth needed to dare release her Fitzwilliam.

"That is impossible, Brother. Miss Bingley is in one guest suite, and George in the other. Your mistress will need to find another home to sully with her recuperation. I never knew you to be so violent, Fitzwilliam." Georgiana's tart reply stung her brother, but he quickly recovered. He looked from the unfamiliar harpy now dwelling in his sweet sibling to the harpy he knew all too well standing just a few steps above her.

With a smirk, Darcy stepped forward so the front door might close properly less all of London be privy to his private nightmare. Pulling his gloves off and handing them to the young footman Jack, Darcy addressed Mrs. Potter, stalled in her progress on the landing for further instructions.

"Please situate Miss Bennet in the mistress chambers." Mrs. Potter beamed at her master, and carefully helped her charge take each step one at a time.

"You're home suddenly, bit brazen to bring your side dish home to London while your wife is in Kent. Didn't think you had in you Darcy."

"Mr. Arthur, gather the strongest footmen you have and throw this man out of my home this instant." Darcy refused to even acknowledge Wickham.

"Fitzwilliam, no! The talk! Not my husband!" Georgiana rushed forward to grab her brother's arm in desperation but Darcy shrugged her off.

"Go with him, you shrew. For shame you would sell your family's belongings for his schemes! For shame! Oh yes, dear sister, I know all, thanks to Mrs. Potter's fast thinking. I have agents scouring dealers all over England to procure our family's treasures. Treasures you are not fit to even gaze upon." Darcy looked to Mr. Arthur, his butler. "Throw him out now, send a stable boy to fetch his things."

Six burly men moved forward as one, gleefully delighted in their assignment. Wickham protested most strenuously, but with his injuries and lack of fitness, he was no match for such numbers.

"Georgie! Georgie! Remember I love you; I've always loved you! Don't let him turn you against me . . ." His cries trailed off the further he was carried off the property.

"How could you!" Georgiana cried, clenching her fists. "You've stayed away all these months, and just show up to throw people out?"

Darcy clasped his sister's tiny weapons and stood shocked that for the first time, he felt nothing towards this young woman. No pangs of reminiscence, no sympathy. "You never came to me for help in anything, don't pretend to need my protection now. You have betrayed this family is so many ways; I no longer trust you. It is beneath me to throw a female relation out, but do not test me."

"You brute! You monster! As if you could control me, I no longer belong to you. I am Mrs. George Wickham!"

"Yes, and your future lies penniless out on the sidewalk, with the muck and the mire. Do chase after him." Darcy released his sister and stepped beyond her, to face the final challenge.

"Mr. Darcy, I am so relieved you are home—" Miss Bingley did not miss an opportunity and descended the stairs with a look of pure triumph on her face.

"Miss Bingley, kindly fetch your brother and sister-in-law if you wish to be of service to my family. As soon as they may be found, if you please."

"But, but, I must speak to you! It is of an urgent nature! I have papers linking your brother-in-law to a scheme involving the Stanley family and mining—"

Darcy stood on the landing, pinching the bridge of his nose as he took every ounce of self-control he had left to thwart this scheming woman's ways. "Miss Bingley, how dense do you believe me to be?"

"Dense? Why no, Mr. Darcy, you are a brilliant business man, my brother says often how well you conduct your holdings and care for so many and I thought a wife of yours should be likewise inclined . . ."

Darcy laughed. Not a light-hearted, polite laugh. But a deep belly rumble as his sister lay pouting on the parquet floor to his right and Charles' sister was again insinuating herself as his future spouse. His heart lay just beyond her, aching with every breath, selfless in her designs to truly care for him.

"Wickham and Stanley conducted their business in MY club. Loyalties to the Darcy family run deep. I've been aware of this scheme for quite some time, needing to wait long enough for the beasts responsible for ruining many an illustrious family to snare their own necks irrevocably in the brambles. Thank you for your interests into my affairs, now kindly fetch your brother or I shall send a servant. It makes no difference to me."

Darcy pushed past the last woman of no consequence to him and thudded up the stairs of his own home, sickened by the clear spaces on the walls where paintings had hung and the outline of the frame stood as a reminder. It was doubtful he would recover all of the items hocked by the Wickhams, but he had no doubts Georgiana was equally responsible for this outright theft.

Reaching his suite, he could hear muffled voices in the mistress wing and was about to enter when Mrs. Potter suddenly exited the room.

"Oh, Mr. Darcy, excuse me, sir."

"How is she? I know she should not have traveled, but the circumstances . . ."

The older woman took pity on her master and tsked, tsked sympathetically. "Her maid told me all about that devil who took his hands to her! She sleeps, we managed to get her to take a dose of laudanum."

"You did? But how?"

Mrs. Potter winked. "Miss Bennet is a remarkable young woman, sir, and sometimes remarkable young men and women need their pride in tact as they are offered a cup of tea."

Darcy smiled in relief, before blowing out a breath. He nodded to his housekeeper and turned around to see to his own care. He had not traveled more than three steps that she called after him.

"Your water be hot, sir. Simmons saw to it right away."

"Thank you, Mrs. Potter." Darcy waved over his shoulder. "If Miss Bingley does not leave in a quarter hour, please send young Calvin to fetch the Bingleys."

"Yes, sir." Mrs. Potter managed before the door to the master's suite shut with a resounding finality. As Catherine Potter turned to go below and see to the kitchens, with her first step she knew without a doubt that with the Master home, soon all would be right as rain once more.

Chapter Thirty-Five

A newly minted master of his own estate, Colonel Richard Fitzwilliam answered his father's beckoning to his own study in a state of great irritation. With the drama of Miss Bennet's injuries and Lady Catherine remaining under Dr. Smeads care and sedation, Rosings had quieted enough that the Earl of Matlock felt confident in explaining to his son how utterly wretched his decision in matrimony had been.

Richard quietly closed the door behind him and called out to his father sitting in the shadows next to the lone fireplace. "I hope you have an important matter to discuss. My wife and I wish for a night of peace."

"Did you care for one moment what your marriage might mean for your family? Or was your selfish disdain merely extended to the tip of your own nose?"

"Careful, Father, careful. I respect your opinion, but I am my own man. You had no qualms about forcing Darcy into this marriage, we merely exchanged one man of Fitzwilliam blood for another."

"Fools! Marriage is not so simple as where you wish to marry, and Darcy will learn first hand when he weds that nothing daughter of some backcountry baronet! There are legal ramifications. Contracts! What settlement did you give Anne? Your paltry Colonel's pay?"

Colonel Fitzwilliam licked his lips and grit his teeth together to bite back his initial reaction. Darcy and he spoke at length how matters were different for their parents; they had no choice. But both men resolved to sow their oats in fields of their own choosing, no matter what the consequences.

"I'm sorry you could not manage your greedy way into my marriage settlement, Father. Perhaps if you had been forthright in your plans I might have considered your wishes into mine. Then again, on second thought, perhaps not." Richard bowed low and attempted to leave but his father cried out. "Our Maker cares not more for an Earl's son or a candlemaker's son when the bullets fly. Good night."

"You would see your mother thrown out? On the streets?"

Richard held up his hand with his back to the Earl. "Do not invoke my mother's security. She and Aunt Catherine may bicker over the Dowager House soon as the renovations are complete. Or are you forgetting my brother?"

"He's not made of your mettle, preferring the company of poets and drunks! The legacy will pass to you undoubtedly when his lifestyle catches up to him. And what legacy will there be? You've placed the land of your ancestors in precarious danger with this foolhardy marriage. Rosings is not but a quarter of Matlock's holdings."

Richard had enough. His leave ended in three days' time and he would need to resign his commission to remain with Anne, but he despised the idea of leaving her, nor could he ask her to travel. He had truly important matters to mind, not the tantrum of a peer.

"Your business dealings are your own, sir. Again, you do not consult me on your own mind, I prefer to keep my own counsel. But don't worry, Father. Pray for the death of your niece and all shall be well. I can still marry that on-the-shelf third daughter of the Duke of Northumberland and his loans will flood your coffers."

"You knew! You ungrateful, spiteful . . ."

The Colonel shrugged and smirked. "I may keep my own counsel from you, but as you point out, Mother and I are very close."

The Earl of Matlock and brother to Lady Catherine de Bourgh was left livid and stewing in his own ire while his son Richard enjoyed the last laugh. In the battles of the generations, he and Darcy had won. This round.

Chapter Thirty-Six

Darcy entered his library with a clear head, clearer than it had been in the last three days. It seemed so long ago that he and Elizabeth were laughing, walking in the meadows of Rosings, delighted with their plans to protect the Holbein family. How his life shifted so dramatically sideways, he did not know, but the pattern of such developments for nearly nine months wore him thin.

Charles Bingley greeted his oldest friend with a genuine embrace, the first time the men had seen one another since one's marriage and the other's downfall.

"Darcy, you look hollow my friend. Let me fetch us both a drink." Charles helped himself

A Virtue of Marriage

to the familiar setting of many an evening visit during his bachelor days.

"You should not have to do that . . ."

"My friend, I am happily, blissfully married. You, on the other hand, have been through hellfire and lived to tell the tale. And I was too stupid to not see that you needed me." Charles lifted his drink in a toast, the only amends both men would make to the breach put between them by Georgiana and Bingley's wedding falling on the same day.

Darcy knocked back the pungent liquid, comforted by the burn down his throat. His mind still felt in a fog over cleaning his house of vermin, and two little mice still schemed, he was sure in a suite above.

"Have you seen Elizabeth?" Darcy asked, earnestly.

Charles nodded slowly and placed his glass on a side table. "I'd say I've never seen her look so poorly, but then again . . ."

"I know, I know . . ." Darcy held up his hands in mock guilt. "Speaking of, would you and Jane be willing to stay here while I ride to Longbourn. I must not wait a moment longer and seek Mr. Bennet's approval for her hand."

Charles Bingley grimaced as he witnessed the full-fledged passion his friend held for his sister-in-law. Where he had no doubt of the love and happy future for two of his favorite people in the world, he also had no doubts as to the reception one Mr. Fitzwilliam Darcy was likely to receive upon visiting Longbourn.

"Perhaps you ought to take a seat."

Darcy blanched, but quickly recovered. "Are you saying you will not aid me? Aid Elizabeth?"

"No, Darcy, take a seat, old man! While you and Elizabeth have had your hands full of plans and pretend weddings, the rest of the world marched forward in time. The gossip, the intrigue . . ."

"All reached Elizabeth's family." Darcy collapsed his face into his hands, propped upon his knees at the elbow.

"I'm afraid so. I endured a ghastly upbraiding the last night we hosted the Bennets in Hertfordshire, I tell you! I'm not sure Mr. Bennet will come around, least not before you are his son-in-law." Bingley retrieved his drink and took a healthy swallow.

Tentatively Darcy looked up from his disgrace. "What do you mean, before I become his son-in-law?"

Charles smiled. Raised his glass to his friend and shrugged. "Last I checked you are master of Pemberley, this home, and Carver House, are you not?"

"Are you suggesting?"

"Jane is upstairs telling her sister the lay of the land as we speak. Now, as Elizabeth's nearest male relation, it might do best if she recovers a week or two before dashing off to Scotland. But, even with my Jane in the family way, she made me swear we would stand beside the two of you at the anvil."

"Bingley, you are a godsend!" Darcy said, rising from his chair.

"What did I do?"

"You and Jane have come through when we've needed you most. She shall never say it, but she needs her family. The breach is killing her inside."

Bingley scratched his head at how much Darcy seemed to know of his future bride when he felt he was learning the inner desires of his actual bride every day. "And what of the house? If Jane and I follow, there will be none to protect your holdings. The Fitzwilliams are all in Kent, are they not?"

Darcy paused at the door and looked back. "The house be damned for all I care! There are more valuables in life all around us too easily lost. I shall not lose her again." Darcy left the library to return back above stairs to see his Elizabeth. With Jane explaining the situation, Darcy was certain his Lizzie needed him without delay.

Chapter Thirty-Seven

Coming upon the sisters in tears, Darcy's plan to provide comfort suddenly felt misapplied. The two women were in an embrace and Darcy felt loathe interrupting them. But when Elizabeth's eyes popped open and she spied her love, she beamed at him and beckoned him closer with her hands behind Jane's back.

"Fitzwilliam, is it true? Shall we leave for Scotland this very moment? I am well, I swear!"

"Oh no, Miss Bennet, I will not fall for those tricks again. You have been moved once at great peril to your health, not again!"

"Lizzie, you do not listen. There must be at least a week before you can travel that distance again. Doctor Matthew's orders." Jane rubbed her midsection absently, warmed that her headstrong sister still needed the gentle guidance here and again.

"But, if we wait too long, you might not be able to travel!"

"I have it on good authority that not only one Bennet sister is stubborn in her travel arrangements in spite of her health." Darcy matched his future wife's arched eyebrows with one of his own, bringing her to a fit of laughter at his comical face.

"Speaking of my husband, perhaps I shall nip downstairs to see how he fares." Jane announced her awarding of privacy to the couple as smoothly as she could manage, and gave her sister another kiss on the cheek and warm hug before rising from the bed.

"Be careful of the stairs!" Elizabeth called earnestly behind her, making Jane turn around shocked that she, the well-behaved sister, should be warned such.

"And you be careful of Mr. Darcy! I'm leaving the door open." Jane announced before leaving.

Darcy wasted no time in rushing to Elizabeth's side, peppering her bruised and battered face with kisses, as he held her head tenderly in his cupped hands. Elizabeth tried to return his passions, but her lips remained off kilter from the minor swelling refusing to abate just yet.

"Is it true? Truly true? Two weeks time and we shall be married?" Elizabeth rushed her words and she panted for air in the crush of Mr. Darcy's arms.

"Truly true. The second you are well, we make haste for the border my love."

Darcy pulled back for a moment and looked down at his beloved's face, refusing to dwell on the ugliness of violence displayed across it. As she began to tear up at such strong emotions, Darcy took a page out of her book.

"And while we may honeymoon at Carver House, I cannot promise there to be a stick of furniture left in the home."

The two laughed and Elizabeth teased her husband for worrying about such frivolous matters. The last reason in the world she was marrying this man was for his furniture!

Chapter Thirty-Eight

Charlotte Collins plucked strawberries from her garden keeping a keen eye out for lizards. The mid-day sun felt relentless on her bare neck and she chided herself for not rising early and picking fruit in the cool morning's shade. A large shadow loomed suddenly over her, blocking out the sun and acted a reminder of her responsibilities.

Sighing, she removed her garden gloves and lifted her basket full of her labors. She was out of time and would not wish to make her visitor wait for all of the world. Squinting up, she looked at the burly man with the sun's intense ray framing his person.

A Virtue of Marriage

"You're so perfectly punctual, Declan, I'm thankful the big house can spare you this afternoon."

"Mrs. Collins, I am happy to be of service." He offered a hand down to assist the woman up, a woman placed directly in his protection from his employer, Colonel Richard Fitzwilliam. Declan took the basket and earned Mrs. Collins' thanks.

"I am so sorry to call on you, but I fear after just two short weeks, my husband has run away again with his ideas and become rather demanding."

Declan grunted, remembering well the squeals of the portly man half his height on the night of retribution for his sins. The joy of inflicting further pain on this excuse for a man delighted the stocky Irishman down to his toes.

"Has the mister been hurting ye?"

"No, no, he knows better, but I thought perhaps a reminder of his new position was in order, if you do not mind. Would you care to stay for luncheon?"

Declan grunted his approval, and followed the petite woman into the cottage, ducking his head to properly enter the doorway.

"Charlotte! Charlotte!" Mr. Collins called out as the door opened, only for a scream best described as a woman's cry left his person and he dropped the post as he covered his mouth.

Declan gave his lopsided grin and took off his simple hat as a sign of respect.

"No, I've not raised a hand to her. I swear! Leave, leave at once. Tell him, Charlotte."

Charlotte looked to her husband trying to hide behind the corner of the wall that led to the kitchens and back to the tall specimen of man standing next to her. A flush of warmth overcame her. Fanning her face from her blush, she beckoned Declan to follow her, thoroughly enjoying the further shirking of Mr. Collins as they approached.

"Oh, Declan is here for luncheon, I thought it would be nice to host company for once. What do you think, William?" Charlotte asked with a fake air of innocence.

William Collins gulped as the man chiefly responsible for the worst thrashing of his life stood not two feet away from him. Only a few days ago, the pastor managed to sit upon his posterior without twinges of pain, and the gash over his forehead from Mr. Darcy's signet ring would likely scar.

"Ye—yes, anything you desire, my dear."

"Perfect! Now, were there any letters for me?"

Collins jumped to collect the post from the floor, scrambling to find the letter for his wife from her friend and his cousin.

Charlotte thanked her husband and tore open the missive.

Dearest Charlotte,

I apologize for not taking my leave of you before departing Kent but I have it on good authority your circumstances are most heartily changed.

Charlotte looked up at poor Declan trying his best to take a graceful seat at her dinning room table. Cook and Eileen brought out the fare, and Charlotte nodded at their perfect manners towards a footman from the main house. There was no mistaking that Declan's position in the Collins' household exceeded his official rank in actual worth.

Wish me luck as I am to board a carriage this very afternoon to hasten to Scotland! Mr. Darcy and I are finally seeking out own destinies, and Jane and Mr. Bingley are to come along!

I confess I am jubilant at finally securing my knight in shining armor. Please pray for my soon to be sisters-in-law. The scandal of Wickham's business dealings are rippling through London and neither Georgiana nor Caroline are seeing many invitations for their company.

I received a lovely gift by way of Jane from Kitty! She has made a portfolio of her art and Mr. Darcy has said we shall invite her and your younger sister, Maria, to Pemberley at the end of this summer. I hope you will consent to a visit as well, though I'm afraid the invitation does not extend to my cousin.

Well, I am off and must send this quickly. All of my love and best wishes, until we see each other again. This is my last letter as . . .

Elizabeth Bennet

Charlotte smiled, refolded the letter and placed the parchment in the pocket of her apron. With luncheon served, before she took a bite, she asked Declan a straightforward question.

"How would you enjoy a trip to Derbyshire this summer, Declan?"

~*fin*~

And off we go to Scotland! The Blessing of Marriage coming June 2015 to all major book retailers!

Visit the *Rose Room,* an exclusive reading club, for more information and to read free stories. Available free at http://elizabethannwest.com/roseroom

ABOUT THE AUTHOR

Elizabeth Ann West is a jane-of-all-trades, mistress to none. Author of the best-selling women's fiction, *Cancelled*, and historical romance series *Seasons of Serendipity*, she began her writing career in 2007 writing advertising copy for websites. Since then, she has learned to make apps, code websites, and make a mean cup of coffee. Originally from Virginia Beach, VA, her family now moves wherever the Navy sends them.

You can contact her atwriter@elizabethannwest.com

Or join her Pemberley Possibilities mailing list:

http://bit.ly/emailpemberley

One of the best parts of being an author is the wonderful men and women working beside you to tell their wonderful stories of Our Dear Couple. Please enjoy the first two chapters of J. Dawn King's A Father's Sins, available in ebook, paperback and in both English and Spanish.

PROLOGUE

November 11, 1805 – Hatchards Book Shop, Piccadilly

Twenty-one year old Fitzwilliam Darcy perused the tall shelves, looking for an intriguing title to add to his growing personal library. The selections appeared endless. Hatchards, one of the more established booksellers in London, had shelves upon shelves filled with first editions and copies of modern and ancient-language manuscripts. Stacks were carefully arranged and displayed on tables to draw the reader's attention. Carefully studying the gold-stamped spines on the leather volumes, he became aware of a melodic voice repeating the words, "they are not to be found", "they are not to be found", with a variation once in a while of "no, they are not to be found".

"I wonder what the lady is looking for," the young man thought. It was rather an odd section of the store to find a female and her voice sounded quite youthful. Unable to stifle his curiosity, he walked to the end of the aisle and peeked around the corner.

He was correct; she was young, possibly in her thirteenth or fourteenth year. Slight of stature, with long, wavy, chocolate-brown hair, she was extended up on her toes with her arms outstretched and her small fingertips trying to reach the top shelf.

"Miss, may I be of some assistance?"

She was so focused on her search, his deep baritone voice startled her and she nearly toppled over. With her hand to her chest, she dropped her heels back to the ground and glanced at the handsome gentleman. Tall, with dark, wavy hair and dark eyes, he was smiling slightly as he stepped closer. She returned his smile with a delightful twinkle in her hazel eyes. "Unless you can miraculously extend my height or shorten the shelves, I am unsure how you may be of help, sir".

Delighted with her countenance and her wit, Darcy did something completely outside his character; he proceeded to converse with a complete stranger. Her clothing proclaimed her, not of the first circle, but certainly a young, gently-born miss; even though not of his sphere. He had finished his first season, which his peers referred to as the "marriage mart" and had become used to ladies of every age, including those far too young to be "out", and their mothers preening and prancing around him trying to attract his attention. This girl did nothing of the sort. "I am terribly sorry, Miss, that I am unable to do either of those tasks." He paused and put his finger to the side of his cheek as if in deep thought. "However, if you would tell me which volume you are so diligently searching for, I would be pleased to help you in your search."

"Thank you, kind sir." Removing a small scrap of paper from her reticule, she read off the journals of four explorers: George Vancouver and his discovery of the North Pacific Ocean, the voyages of Captain James Cook, and Meriwether Lewis and William Clark of the American expedition. "Do you know where I might find any of these books?"

"Yes, miss, I do know of these writings." Again, he paused as if in thought.

"Sir, are you uncertain as to how to tell me their location?" She raised one eyebrow and smiled again. Looking closer at the man, she found him to have such a pleasant face. Relaxed and contented.

He looked down at her and his smile grew. For someone so young, her eyes sparkled with life and joy. "The first books you asked for, the journals of Vancouver, I have read myself. They are located…" reaching up, he easily found the three volumes from the top shelf just an arm length from where he was standing …"here". Before he handed them to her, he turned back to the young girl to get her attention. "Nonetheless, I am saddened to tell you that the journals of Captain Cook and those of the American adventurers have not yet been published. I, too, am anticipating their arrival. I do believe that Mr. Lewis and Mr. Clark have yet to finish their expedition, so it might be a length of time before we are able to read of their activities." He bowed slightly, "I am sorry to disappoint."

"Please do not be concerned." The young lady reached for the three books that were in his hands. "I so enjoy learning of different parts of the world and have a longing to travel to all the remote places I read about. My father teases that I would rather have geography books and old maps than ribbons. He knows me well." She still held out her hands, but he refused to place the volumes there. Instead, he turned and walked up to the shop assistant and set the books on the counter.

When the owner saw the man standing at the counter, he quickly pushed the assistant to the side and inquired of Mr. Darcy how he might help him. "Please wrap these up for the young miss." Without thought as to the propriety of the situation, he proceeded with the transaction as he would with his 9-year-old sister, Georgiana.

"Sir!" interjected the girl, quickly glancing toward the door to see if her uncle's maid, who accompanied her to the store, noticed the exchange. "I am prepared to settle my own account." Turning to the proprietor, she directed, "Before they are wrapped, if I may, I would be most pleased to record my name and today's date on the inside, as I want all to know that they belong to me." Her brilliant smile moved the man to action. While the man obtained quill and ink, Darcy remained at her side. Carefully and methodically, she wrote in a lovely swirl, "Elizabeth Anne Bennet – November 11 in the year 1805."

As the owner, after waiting for the ink to dry, wrapped and tied the books, the two young people stood in silence, he thinking, "her name is Elizabeth Bennet", and she thinking, "he is Mr. Darcy."

One year to the day later - November 11, 1806

Longbourn, Hertfordshire

Thomas Bennet stood and shook with rage. "Pack your things and go!" His face purple with heightened emotions, he pointed his index finger to his once beloved daughter, Elizabeth, and shouted, "I have never been as disappointed in another human soul in my entire life as I am with you, Elizabeth Anne!" He turned to leave his young son's room. Glancing back from the doorway, his pain and grief poured out of him as he shouted once more at her, "You have stolen my future, my dreams, and my family from me and I NEVER want to see your face again!"

The grief Elizabeth felt as she watched her father storm away was almost more than she could endure. Head bowed, tears ran down her cheeks, dropping into a puddle on her lap. Turning to her dear little brother, his lifeless body still on the bed, she gathered him to her 15-year-old breast to snuggle one last time. She had done all she knew to do for the fever, the pain, and the pustules infecting her brother and three younger sisters. With no apothecary to lend them aid, the nursing had fallen to her. Elizabeth's older sister, Jane, had not the emotional fortitude to tend her siblings. Her mother had taken to her bed with a case of nerves at the first sign of the outbreak. The smallpox had devastated the small village of

Longbourn and the surrounding area. While in London visiting their Uncle and Aunt Gardiner, the two oldest Bennet siblings had been inoculated with the vaccine, developed over 10 years before by Dr. Edward Jenner, but the single pox scar left on Elizabeth's right temple persuaded Mrs. Bennet to not allow her youngest three daughters, Mary, Kitty and Lydia, and her only son and heir, Thomas James Bennet to receive the needed medicine. Mrs. Bennet would do anything to not have her most precious offspring marred by such scarring. Satirical cartoons depicting people turning into animals after receiving the vaccine fed her fears. How senseless that had been! Her husband, always longing for peace, to the exclusion of all rational thought, went along with the constantly expressed opinions of his wife. Her father's blame for something that Elizabeth was unable to control added to the agony in her heart for her beloved little brother. To lose little Thomas, her dear sisters, and many of her friends and acquaintances in such a short period was a devastating blow. Then, to have her father unfairly place the blame on her young shoulders was a weight she did not think she was able to bear.

Descending the stairs to the hallway, Elizabeth noticed her sister, Jane, hovering in the doorway of the front parlor. Tears streamed down Jane's face as she wordlessly transmitted the pain and anguish for all they were losing that day. The orders from their father had been clear. Not a word to Elizabeth. No acknowledgement that she existed. Elizabeth gathered her small valise containing her meager possessions and turned to the door.

Hill, the Bennet's longtime butler, took the valise from Elizabeth's small hands. He handed her a sealed letter and then reached into his pockets to retrieve a few shillings that always jingled there. Pressing them into Elizabeth's hands, he sighed deeply, "I only wish it were more, Miss." His beloved Elizabeth glanced up and gave him a tearful smile. "It should see you to your uncle's house in Cheapside." He continued, "May God be with you."

Reaching back, Elizabeth removed the garnet necklace that had been a gift from her father. She dropped it into Hill's hands. With a final sob, Elizabeth Anne Bennet walked away from her home, not looking back.

November 11, 1806 – later that same day

Pemberley Chapel, Derbyshire

The young man stood in front of the family crypt in the chapel, his head hanging in silent grief; his ten-year-old sister crying silently beside him. It had been unexpected, their father's death. The pain of their loss was sharpened by the whispers from their neighbors in the chapel, from the servants that wandered through the hallways and rooms of their home, and from the distant Darcy family that came at the first news of distress. "Who will be the new master of Pemberley?"

Running his long fingers over the name engraved on the tomb next to the newly opened vault, he read aloud, "Anne Fitzwilliam Darcy". Before the week was out, the name "George Adam Darcy" would be carved next to his neighbor. Truly, they were now closer in death than Fitzwilliam Darcy had ever seen them in life.

"Come, dear Georgie, let us return." His little sister remained unmoved. He bent and lifted her, holding her close, carrying her to the carriage that waited outside the chapel. He did not see the craftsmen waiting to finish their job. Nor did he see the other mourners gathered in clumps, their own eyes trained on Mr. Darcy's second son. But, he heard the whispers. "Who will be the new master of Pemberley?"

CHAPTER ONE

Five Years Later – November 10, 1811 - Officer's Quarters – Meryton, Hertfordshire

The two handsome, young gentlemen mounted their waiting horses outside the officer's dining hall. "Darcy, I just do not understand how you can be uncomfortable in such excellent company. The officer's were pleasant, the food was tolerable, and the stories were entertaining." Charles Bingley shook his head at his friend. They turned their horses and headed to Bingley's leased estate, Netherfield Park.

"I had no prior acquaintance with any of the men, Bingley." Mr. Fitzwilliam Darcy was a private man; taciturn by nature, who did not make friends easily. They were an odd combination; Bingley with his ready smile and pleasant outlook and Darcy with his brooding stare and rigid posture. Darcy's manner did not invite approach. The fortnight they had been in Hertfordshire, Bingley had accepted all manner of invitations: card parties, public assemblies, dinners, and musical evenings where little talent was displayed. It had been a frustration to the ever unsocial Darcy. Bingley was delighted with the country society.

"Well, no matter," Bingley grinned. "We have had pleasant company at home. Miss Jane

Bennet was to have tea with my sisters and I long for a report of her visit." He had a dreamy look on his face. "She is an angel, Darcy, an absolute angel."

The Following Morning

Gracechurch Street – London

Breakfast in the Gardiner household was a family affair. Two times each day the family would gather for a meal and conversation which centered on the news, plans for the day, and hopes for the future. Elizabeth loved her two cousins fiercely and viewed her beloved aunt and uncle as the best examples of reasonable, thinking, gentle people. Her uncle, Mr. Edward Gardiner, had a large import/export business with warehouses in the Cheapside district of London. They were convenient to his home. His wife, Madeline, was kind, intelligent, deeply in love with her husband, and a true partner in every sense in the marriage.

Having lived with the family for the past five years since her abrupt removal from the home she had grown up in, she delighted to see how her 12-year-old cousin, Michael, and his 10-year-old sister, Marie, were involved in these family discussions. Young opinions were sought after, listened to, and reviewed with the weight usually given to learned adults. It was an atmosphere rich in love and intelligence and Elizabeth thrived along with her cousins.

Four of those five years had been spent in travel, expanding business contacts in the international markets. It was a half a year's journey along established trade routes to reach India, a country of diverse cultures, rich in gemstones, spices, silk, cotton, indigo dye, tea, and other items demanded by the wealthy matrons and peers of British society. The return trip, after a stay of just over a year, included stops in other areas abounding in resources; ports on the African coast that supplemented the spices already contracted for in the Indian cities of Calcutta, Bombay, and Madras, stops in the Mediterranean for fine wines, glassware, delicate fabrics, leather goods, and metals, and a final stop in Portugal for the most desired port wines and lacework. Business had been brisk and the adventure, the different climates and cultures, the variety of peoples thrilled young Elizabeth as she broadened the scope of her known world.

Visiting Verona, she could not help but imagine herself as Shakespeare's Juliet Capulet on a medieval balcony in a lovely courtyard awaiting her lover, Romeo. In Venice, she was on constant lookout for Shylock, the Jewish moneylender in Merchant of Venice, and in

Rome, while touring the ruins of the ancient Holy Roman Empire, she imagined happening upon members of the Roman Senate or one of the Caesars wearing a toga or a Cardinal in their clothes of state. In Athens, while her uncle visited warehouses, she and her cousins and aunt toured the ancient buildings and temples that housed the gods and goddesses that had so enraptured her when she had listened to her father read Homer's Odyssey and other classics in their original languages so many years ago. Finally, in Egypt, she imagined Queen Cleopatra and her consort, Marc Antony, resting on a barge as they floated the river Nile, just as the whole Gardiner family had opportunity to do. The ancient pyramids were impressive in their grandeur and the only regret Elizabeth had was that she could not share these wondrous experiences with her father.

As this thought filtered through her mind, Elizabeth forced it back into the obscure recesses where it belonged. The continued animosity of her father no longer weighed as heavily on her heart as it had five years previously. An irregular correspondence with her old friend and neighbor, Charlotte Lucas, warned her that the same attitude prevailed over Longbourn, as it had five years previously. During the lengthy travels, Elizabeth took opportunity, especially in India where they had long felt the ravages of smallpox, to learn as much as possible about treatment and prevention of many diseases. She kept a journal, not only of the places she saw and the people she met, but also included step-by-step preparations for many preventatives and treatments available with the wider variety of herbs, plants, and organics native to the areas she visited. Not gifted or trained in drawing or painting, she endeavored to search out other young ladies skilled in those arts to illustrate these journals. At her uncle's suggestion, she also collected vials and samples to carry back to England for any future use. It was a comprehensive collection and very much treasured by the entire family. Elizabeth also included in the journal recipes and instructions for the many different foods they had sampled. It had been a wonderful journey.

It had taken the three months they had been back in England to determine a proper location for the many remembrances they had brought back and to establish a routine that the Gardiners would cling to for the rest of their married life. The movement and sounds of the ship, the creaking of the wooden hull, the snapping of the sails, the calls of crewmembers from one to another, were now just a pleasant memory. Hearing English spoken was no longer a longed-for novelty, but was now expected. The sights and smells of London, even those upon their arrival in the sweltering August temperatures, were welcome to the weary travelers.

After breaking her fast with the rest of the family, Elizabeth settled into the large, overstuffed chair in her aunt's smallest sitting room to finish a needlework project. Thinking of the changes that the past years had brought stimulated her thinking as to what the future might hold. She set her embroidery down on her lap, pondering other journeys that would be pleasurable; the Americas, the South Pacific, or the Orient. Elizabeth was well aware that her uncle and aunt had allowed her many freedoms not typical of a girl her age. In just over seven months she would reach her majority and have the decision as to what her future would be. She had diligently saved any spending allowance given her by her uncle, being frugal in her purchases. Her uncle then invested her meager funds until she had some savings; which she kept in a drawer by her bedside. Elizabeth was just tying off a thread when a footman entered. "An express for you, Miss. The rider is waiting for a reply."

"An express letter? For me?" She had never received any post by express. Charlotte was her only correspondent. For someone to go to this expense, it had to be either the best of news or the worst of news. Before she could lay claim to the missive, the butler, Mr. Harrison, walked up behind the footman. "Miss Elizabeth, another express rider has just arrived and he has another letter for you."

This was clearly too much. "Please, Mr. Harrison, send for my aunt and uncle. I fear this news." Mr. Harrison and the footman retreated immediately.

While she waited for the Gardiners, she thought back to Charlotte's last letter. There had been much news from the area of Meryton. She had written that after years of vacancy, Netherfield Park had been let at last by a young, single man from the north who had family members and close friends in residence with him for the past fortnight. According to Charlotte, the young man was handsome, friendly, rich, and enthusiastically pursuing 23-year-old Jane Bennet. A Mr. Charles Bingley, she noted. In other news, Charlotte's younger brother, Mr. Robert Lucas, had just returned from his studies in Cambridge and would be taking over the responsibilities of stewardship of Lucas Lodge from his father, Sir William Lucas. And the militia was coming to Meryton. Elizabeth considered how pleased her mother must be with those circumstances. Single gentlemen in the neighborhood would be viewed as a gift from God to all mothers with unmarried daughters. Charlotte had also mentioned that the heir to Elizabeth's former home, Mr. William Collins, was due for a lengthy visit to Longbourn. Mrs.

Bennet had told Lady Lucas, Charlotte's mother, that they were not looking forward to the visit, as she felt he was there to determine Mr. Bennet's health and project when and if he might inherit soon. It must certainly be a distasteful prospect. Elizabeth did not recall if Charlotte mentioned when her father's cousin was due to arrive.

Her aunt and uncle entered the room together. Both showed deep concern on their faces. Mr. Gardiner took the two letters from the butler and examined the addresses on the outside before suggesting that the two ladies be seated. Anxiety, suspense, and trepidation radiated from Elizabeth's eyes as her gaze focused entirely on her uncle. Unnoticed was the retreat of the servants, the voices of the cousins from the library, the firelight flickering in the fireplace in the wall by the window, and the branches of the tree outside the window tapping against the glass in the wind.

"Uncle?"

"Yes, Lizzy," he glanced down at the letters again. "It appears that one originated from Netherfield Park and the other is from your father." Both he and his wife looked to see Elizabeth's reaction to this stunning news. Longbourn. It had been five long years since she had had any contact with her family. Elizabeth always asked of the family when she wrote to Charlotte, but the replies were always the same, brief and vague. They were enough to let Elizabeth know that the circumstances and attitudes were unchanged. Therefore, the news could not be good. The residents of Netherfield Park were unknown to her and she could not begin to wonder who or what that missive might contain. How and why did they contact her, and by express? Strong emotions roiled in Elizabeth's mind and heart, making her breathing shallow and causing the blood to rush from her face. "Please, Uncle, please read the post from Netherfield Park. I am all curiosity."

November 11, 1811

Netherfield Park, Hertfordshire

Dear Miss Elizabeth Bennet,

Please pardon this lapse in propriety for writing when we have not been properly introduced. I am Miss Georgiana Darcy. My brother and I are guests of Mr. Charles Bingley and his two sisters, Mrs. Louisa Hurst and Miss Caroline Bingley.

Yesterday, your sister, Miss Jane Bennet, was invited to tea. Shortly after her arrival, she became ill and I am sorry to tell you that her condition has worsened. We applied to Longbourn for assistance, but received a return note that Miss Bennet would need to remain here at Netherfield Park. As you may be aware, there is no apothecary or surgeon available in the area. Throughout the night, your sister called for you.

My brother, Fitzwilliam Darcy, happened upon Miss Charlotte Lucas this morning as he rode to Meryton seeking medical help and she gave him your directions. My brother and I, along with Mr. Bingley, feel that Miss Bennet will not improve without you by her side. Please accept this plea from strangers as an expression of sincere concern for your sister's health.

If you require assistance in travel, please advise the express rider, as he is to wait for a response and is authorized to assist you in any way you require. Mr. Bingley has offered lodging here at Netherfield Park for as long as you need. Please come soon.

Yours respectfully,

Miss Georgiana Darcy

Elizabeth had not realized she had been holding her breath the whole time her uncle read. "Oh, poor Jane," she thought as she slowly released the air from her lungs. Her sharp mind quickly assumed that her father's express must contain the same news. "I must go immediately." She rose at the same time as her aunt and they quickly climbed the stairs to the family quarters to pack the few items she would need to travel to Hertfordshire.

Mr. Gardiner ordered the carriage to be brought around and offered the post rider sustenance in the kitchen while they waited. As he stood in the hallway, listening to the increased activity, he mindlessly broke the seal on the remaining letter. The note from Thomas Bennet was brief and abrupt. It was a summons. A summons to Longbourn. After five long years, this was entirely unexpected and would come as a shock to Elizabeth. He walked back to the sitting room as he heard his wife and niece descend the staircase. Taking a seat, he waited, listening to Madeline's final instructions and smiling slightly at the close bond between the two women. This was going to be hard on both of them. And it was hard on him. He loved his niece as if she were one of his own. In the years they had traveled together, Elizabeth had proved to be the best of companions to the whole Gardiner family. She enthusiastically accepted each adventure and gloried in meeting new people and seeing new things. She enjoyed learning, both by reading and study, and by experiencing whatever life had to offer. It had taken many months after first arriving in London for her to let go of the resentment she had of her parents and recapture the joy of life that was her character. At times, melancholy set in. The autumn and beginning of the winter months were particularly hard, as it was at this time of the year that the Bennet family had suffered the loss of four children, in particular, the heir. Mr. Gardiner shook his head as he looked unseeingly at the floor. How Thomas Bennet could possibly blame his own, favorite daughter for deaths that he himself had done nothing to prevent was far beyond the thinking of his brother-in-law.

It had taken years for Elizabeth to face some hard truths about her father. Her love no longer blinded her to his utter selfishness and his lack of concern for even his closest family members. He had been a poor master of Longbourn estate until he had a son. The entail was then broken and he had then resolved to invest his time and effort to establish an inheritance worthy of the new heir. His habitual self-indulgent, self-involved lifestyle was gone as he closely reviewed account books and discussed crops, saw to needed repairs, and tried to rebuild relations with the tenants that worked to support Longbourn. All of his efforts ended when little Thomas James succumbed to the plague. It truly was not his nature to accept responsibility for his own failure. He needed someone to blame and that someone was the only person that had worked tirelessly to try to bring some comfort to those ailing. It had taken years to release the weight of that blame from her slender shoulders; a blame that never should have been there in the first place.

Madeline and Elizabeth entered the room as the butler announced the carriage was waiting and the post rider was ready to leave. "One moment, please." Mr. Gardiner looked at the two women. "I need to have a word with my wife and niece." Mr. Harrison backed out of the room and closed the door. "Please sit for a moment."

As they sat together on the settee, Mr. Gardiner closely observed Elizabeth as he held up her father's note. "Lizzy, you need to hear this. I don't believe any of us thought that it might be any different from Miss Darcy's letter. Yet, why he would want you to nurse your only surviving sister after the blame he carries for you in the loss of your siblings should have prompted us to believe differently." He paused to see if Elizabeth caught his meaning. Observing her close attention, he volunteered to read its contents aloud.

November 11, 1811

Longbourn

Miss Elizabeth Anne Bennet,

It has come to my attention, from speaking with Miss Lucas, that you are at this time unwed. My cousin, the heir to Longbourn, is in residence and desires to marry into the family, so as not to inconvenience your mother by turning her out of her home upon my eventual passing. Therefore, I have arranged for your betrothal and demand you return to Longbourn immediately to be wed. The first of the banns will be read Sunday next and the wedding will take place in four weeks. It is the least you can do for the harm you have caused this family.

Mr. Thomas Bennet

Silence filled the room. The hush seemed to last indefinitely. "Uncle, can my father do this to me? Does he still have authority? What am I to do?" The questions fired rapidly from Elizabeth. Her mind was swirling with the need to know immediately where she stood. When she had left Longbourn all those years ago, she had assumed the letter that had been handed her by Hill was written by her father to her uncle, assigning him all rights and authority over her. He stated clearly, she thought, that she was no longer considered his offspring. Elizabeth was now just twenty years old and would not reach her majority for almost another year. "Uncle?" she said into the quiet.

Anger poured from Mr. Gardiner. He wondered to himself how his intelligent, educated brother–in-law could possibly continue to blame Elizabeth for a poor decision he had made to not have his other children protected from harm. Thomas Bennet's failure to accept responsibility and to pass the blame on to another reflected poorly on the Bennet name. His passing the blame on to a beloved, favorite daughter was unconscionable. "I do not know, Lizzy. I shall have to contact our solicitor, Mr. Haggerston, to find out if Bennet has the right to sign a marriage contract in your behalf and whether you are legally obligated to follow through with this wedding. I shall write for an appointment immediately and send the answers Mr. Haggerston provides to you at Netherfield Park. Do you have all you need for your travels?"

Thinking of the apothecary case with the herbs and tinctures mixed and ready for use, her two journals, one with the notes from her study of the healing arts and the other she kept of their ocean voyages, the few precious volumes she had collected that Jane might find intriguing to read while she recovered.... if she recovered... and her personal items, she felt she was as ready as could be. Her uncle and aunt looked at the small valise and realized their niece had no idea as to staying in Hertfordshire for any longer than necessary, and nodded to one another in understanding. She would be back in London with them soon. Mr. Gardiner took a small purse with coins from his pocket and pressed it into Elizabeth's hands. "Just in case, dear, just in case."

Climbing into the carriage, Elizabeth watched her beloved relatives as long as possible and wondered what changes in her life this return to Hertfordshire might bring. As the carriage wound through the neighborhoods leading from her home to an unanticipated and unexpected destination, she pondered the differences in her thoughts and emotions from now to what they had been five years ago. She had left Hertfordshire a young, naïve, trusting girl and was returning as a woman of the world; older, knowledgeable of so many different things that she never could have learned in her home county, and experienced in being part of a loving, welcoming family. She was not the same person as before, so it was only reasonable to assume that her family and neighbors had changed as well. Setting aside the pain of the summons from her father and her deep concern for the health of her sister, she determined that she would find some morsel of education or enjoyment from this experience and anticipated meeting the residents and guests of Netherfield Park. Possibly, she may have opportunity to again see her beloved friend Charlotte. Elizabeth pondered on Miss Georgiana Darcy and her brother, Mr. Fitzwilliam Darcy. Their last name conjured up an image of the pleasant young man she had briefly conversed with in the bookstore all of those years ago. She wondered if he was family to the brother or sister staying in Hertfordshire. Elizabeth settled back into the cushions of the carriage and thought about what possibilities her future might hold.

***

You can pick up your copy of *A Father's Sins* by J Dawn King at all major retailers!

Made in the USA
Middletown, DE
25 September 2015